I'm a Therapist, and My Patient is Going to be the Next School Shooter

6 Patient Files That Will Keep You Up at Night

Dr. Harper

This is a work of fiction.

Names, characters, businesses, places, events, locales, and incidents are either the products of the author's imagination or used in a fictitious manner.

Any resemblance to actual persons, living or dead, or actual events is purely coincidental.

DEDICATION

These patient files are dedicated to the readers of
/r/nosleep. Thank you for bringing these stories to life.

Thank you to Sachi Amanze for creating the beautiful
illustrations at the start of each patient file. Check out
more of Sachi's work on Instagram: @soliviaam

Thank you to Emmett Doane for creating the final
"photo" that captured our hearts. Check out more of
Emmett's work on Instagram: @mothflowerss

Thank you to the moderators and users of the subreddit
and Discord server. You made this such a fun experience.

And finally, a special thank you to my one and only
beta reader. I love you.

MY PATIENTS

In this folder, I have shared six of my most dangerous patient files. They are not necessarily in chronological order, but they are in the order you should read them.

At the end of each patient file, I've included small notes to provide you with more details. I apologize in advance for all of my doodling. It's just how I remember some of the events and people involved.

Keep in mind, I chose these six patient files for one very important reason: They all lead up to Patient #220 — the patient who ruined someone's life forever.

PATIENT FILES

School Shooter   1

OCD Rituals   21

Choir Boy   55

PTSD Nightmares   71

Abusive Couple   95

Patient #220   123

School Shooter

School Shooter

PART ONE

I've been treating Alex for almost a year now, but the vague threats started around Thanksgiving.

He'd fallen in love with a girl named Emma, and she didn't feel the same way. Typical high school heartbreak. The problem was, he wouldn't back off. He kept asking her out, and she kept rejecting him.

He ranted about her every week – she didn't appreciate him, she led him on, her friends mocked him, etc.

I gently suggested that he give her some space, and he burst into a grandiose tirade about how all women are sluts.

This wasn't the first time he's gotten angry. That's why his mom sent him to me in the first place. He had a history of outbursts and antisocial behavior, which led to other students alienating him.

But this *was* the first time I felt afraid of Alex. There was a frenzied look in his eyes, like he wasn't really in control anymore. And it wasn't just anger. It was elation.

When he came back the next week, he seemed much calmer, but that only made me more uncomfortable. I tried to casually comment that he seemed happier this week, and he told me that he had "figured it all out".

I asked him what that meant, and his only response was a slight smirk.

You know that feeling in your gut, when you know something is terribly wrong, but you don't want to believe it?

That's the feeling that keeps me up at night.

A few months ago, Alex was just an agitated teenager who struggled with making friends. He carried a lot of rage about his dad abandoning his family, but people can work through that stuff. That's what I'm here for.

But now we're in a whole different realm.

In last Wednesday's session, I did something I'm not proud of. Something that could cost me my job. I asked the school receptionist to interrupt our session and bring Alex outside for a phone call.

The moment he left, I reached for his backpack and started digging. Regular stuff, like notebooks and binders. I flipped through the pages and found nothing but doodles and notes.

What was I doing?

I stuck my hand deeper into the bag and felt something. It was one of those old TI graphic calculators. I slid off the cover and tried my hardest to remember my Algebra days from high school.

PRGRM. That's where we used to goof around.

The first program was called EMMA. I opened it up, heart pounding:

1. WHO
2. WHERE
3. WHEN

I pressed (1)

Emma, Christine, Sara, Chris. After that, as many as possible. Need 20+ for top 10.

Then I pressed (2)

Probably chemistry. Maybe the library, when she's on her free period with the other bitches.

And finally (3)

December 17. Right before Christmas, like Newtown. Ruins the holiday for everyone.

Hands sweating, I reached for my phone to take a photo. And that's when the door opened.

"What are you doing?" Alex lunged forward and grabbed the calculator.

"Alex, we need to—"

"You can't go through my stuff," he mumbled. Then he packed his bag and stormed out of the room.

Shit. I thought to myself. *Shit, shit, shit.*

I called the police first. They came over to interview me and said they'd take the report very seriously. They asked if I took photos of the calculator. Nope. Five more seconds would have made all the difference.

Then I talked with the school. They said they'd work with the police to investigate.

But last night, the police informed me that they had completed their investigation and found nothing of concern.

Of course they didn't. Alex knew I'd report him, so he hid everything. *Shit.*

We have our next session tomorrow — the last one before December 17.

He still hasn't canceled.

3

PART TWO

What would you do if someone told you about 9/11 the day before it happened? Or Newtown? Or Vegas?

How would you stop it, without sounding like a raving lunatic?

Maybe you'd suggest I contact Alex's mom. I tried, and she told me to back off or she'd get a restraining order.

Maybe you'd suggest that I'm terrible at my job, and that I should refer him to someone else. I don't blame you. Just wait until you hear about my other patients.

Maybe you'd suggest a 5150 (involuntary hospitalization). Probably the best idea, but I'm a control freak, and I think I know more about Alex than anyone could learn in 72 hours. Involuntary *anything* would only worsen his state.

Maybe you'd suggest I kill him. I'll be honest, it crossed my mind. Not my proudest moment.

Maybe you'd suggest I stay home today, but I couldn't do it. I couldn't be the next therapist or neighbor or friend in the news, reminiscing about all the warning signs, and how the tragedy could have been prevented.

Not when kids were in danger.

To the school's credit, they hired two armed resource officers, and both of them stood outside my office while Alex and I sat down for our session.

Given the circumstances, I actually couldn't have felt more relaxed. They already patted him down and took his bag. Plus, every second that Alex spent in here meant he wasn't out there.

"Alex," I began. "We need to talk about what happened last week."

His head was down and he didn't speak.

"You didn't cancel our session," I said. " Your mom didn't even want you here, but you still came. I have to assume that means you're having second thoughts?"

Alex looked up, but didn't make eye contact. "I'm not saying anything about last week," he said. "I know you probably set up cameras."

My stomach turned. He wasn't wrong.

"Okay," I said. "What if we talk about something else then?"

"Like what?"

I bit my lip and decided to go for it. "Your dad."

Finally, his eyes met mine. They were bloodshot, wide, and exhausted.

"What about him?"

"He left a long time ago, Alex," I said. "But I think the pain still lives inside you."

"I don't have any pain," he spat. "I'm glad the asshole's gone."

"What about Emma?" I asked. "When she rejected you, it caused you so much pain. I saw it all month. You were hurting, Alex."

"*I don't have pain!*" he gripped his chair. "She's just some dumb bitch. I don't give a fuck what she thinks."

"Anger is a totally normal reaction to pain," I said. "Especially recurring pain."

"Would you shut the fuck up about *pain!*" He stood up. "I'm a million times better than Emma and my dad – and fucking *you*."

I took a deep breath and remained seated. "What about the emptiness? The boredom? The loneliness?"

"What?" He was still standing, but he looked like a caged animal. "What are you talking about?"

"Every day, you feel empty," I said. "Disconnected from the world and people around you. Like there's no point to it all. What if we could change that?"

His face went pink and he finally lowered his voice a bit. "We can't."

5

"Of course we can," I said. "Countless people before you have suffered from these wounds, and countless people have healed them."

"Hallmark bullshit."

I bit my lip again. *Shit*, why did I do that? Therapists shouldn't have nervous tics.

"Even if this whole world was pointless and fake, how would harming others help?"

"They deserve it," he said. "They're bullies. They treat me like I'm nobody."

"Sometimes, when we're carrying around abandonment and rejection, we just keep finding more of it," I said. "But Emma isn't a bully for not wanting a relationship. So what could you gain from hurting her and her friends?"

He thought for a moment and said, "I'd be their God for a day."

"But that's no way to gain power and fame," I said. "I mean, no one even remembers the names of the shooters after Parkland. We're numb to it by this point."

He frowned and moved his mouth slightly. I could tell he was trying to prove me wrong, but he couldn't.

"All I'm asking is that you give my way a chance." I leaned forward. "We can turn that emptiness into wholeness. The disconnection into connection. What do you have to lose?"

He paced around the room without speaking for what felt like an eternity.

Finally he came to a stop, and I heard him mumble, "Okay."

My heart flooded with relief. I had just shoehorned his yearlong treatment plan into a 5-minute session, but at least we were getting somewhere.

Then he added, "But—"

No buts. Please. "Alex, I'm fully committed to helping you get to that point," I interrupted before he could change his mind. "But a quick session like this isn't enough to resolve lifelong damage. Maybe you're feeling hopeful now, but that could change tonight, or tomorrow, or next week."

"What are you saying?"

I looked him in the eyes. "I need you under 24x7 supervision," I said. "Would you be willing to agree to voluntary hospitalization? I'll take time away from school to spend every second with you. To help you feel good again."

He glanced at the ground, and then the door. "It won't make any difference."

"Of course it will," I said. "We'll–"

"No, I mean... I'm not the one you need to lock up anymore."

I frowned. "What do you mean?"

"Obviously I wasn't going to get guns inside the school with the guards tailing me," he said. "So we changed the plan after you found the calculator."

"What?" I shook my head. "Alex, who's 'we'? What plan?"

"I'm just supposed to distract you and keep all the guards on this side of the building."

"Distract?" I repeated, heart pounding. "From what?"

"Until he gets to the library."

Before the words came out of his mouth, I bolted up and ran for the fire alarm.

But the sirens were already singing.

PART THREE

A few weeks later, once they moved the bodies and resumed classes, I started clearing out my desk.

Yeah, I got fired.

They always fire the therapist when stuff like this happens. "Should have seen it coming," they say. "All the signs were there."

No kidding.

But it's the school's reason for termination that still burns in my mind: "Reckless behavior resulted in needless tragedy."

It almost sounded like the whole thing was *my* fault.

Maybe I was reckless, I don't know. Sure, it was the opposite of what you're supposed to do in an active shooter situation. But at least I tried.

If you really want to know what happened after the fire alarm went off, I've shared my version of events below. But as you're already quite aware, it's not a happy ending.

"Call him," I said.

"What?" Alex raised his eyebrows.

"If you really want to stop this, take out your phone and call him."

He looked hesitant, but he took out his phone. "What am I supposed to say?"

"Tell him you escaped with one of the officer's guns, and you want him to wait for you – to join in the fun."

The last part made me sick to say, but this had to sound real.

"That's crazy–"

"NOW, Alex."

Just as he held up the phone to his ear, one of the resource officers burst into the room. I hurried over to him and whispered, "It's not Alex."

"What?"

"There's a second shooter," I said, as Alex mumbled into his phone. "You need to be quiet and let him make this call."

"No, I – I can't do that." He stepped forward, but he looked terrified. "We need to wait for the police."

I moved in his way. "Listen. At best, the library is a sixty second sprint from here. How many unarmed students can a gunman kill in one minute?"

He looked around the room nervously.

"Alex is just buying time," I said. "Every second counts. You need to trust me. I know him."

He took a deep breath and gave me a small nod. I think he was actually relieved that I was taking charge, so he didn't have to. I could tell it was taking every ounce of courage he had not to run away.

I glanced at his badge and said, "Dave, I want you to listen to me, okay? Everything is going to be okay."

He nodded again.

"Dave, where is the other officer?"

"I don't– " he trembled. "I don't know."

"Jesus," I muttered under my breath. "You've called 911, right?"

"Yes," he said. "They're three minutes away."

I shook my head. "That's too long."

I turned back to Alex and he was already off the phone. I missed the whole conversation. *Shit.*

"Did he believe you?" I asked.

"I think so," said Alex. "He said he's holding twelve in the library."

I closed my eyes for a moment and turned to the officer. "I need you to give me your gun."

"What?" He shook his head. "No way. What if the kid gets it?"

"Take out the magazine and give me the gun," I repeated.

"N–No. We need to wait for the police and hostage negotiators."

"For fuck's sake, this isn't a hostage situation," I snapped. "It's a massacre, waiting for Player 2 to enter the stage. The second he thinks Alex isn't coming, he'll kill them all."

"But—"

"Jesus, do you want to be the next Parkland guard, like your missing buddy? World famous for letting innocent kids die?"

His face went white.

Finally. Something resonated with him. It's hard to manipulate people you've never met, but that one seemed to hit the mark.

He shook his head, removed the magazine, and handed over the gun.

"Thank you," I said.

I took the gun and shoved it in Alex's hands.

"What the fuck?" Alex and the guard spoke at the same time.

"We're going to the library," I said.

"Why?"

"Alex, right now, you're the only thing keeping those kids alive. As long as he believes you're coming, he won't hurt them. So he has to believe you got the gun."

He swallowed and accepted the gun.

"Good," I said. "Now let's go."

We hurried past the guard, who didn't move or speak another word. It was probably for the best. An officer would only provoke this guy – whoever he was.

As we broke into a run, I said: "Alex, point the gun to my head."

"What? You're nuts."

"Do it," I said. "If he's watching the security feed, this has to look real."

He did as I said. We ran through the hallway as the alarm blared: *Active shooter… This is not a drill… Take cover…*

Now, I had just sixty seconds to figure out two things:

1. Who was the other kid? And what did I need to know

10

about him in order to manipulate him?

2. Did Alex really want to stop this, or was he still playing me? He was clearly capable of fooling me, but I really felt like his breakthrough earlier was genuine. Or maybe that was all just part of the distraction. But he told me about the distraction *before* the alarm went off.

"Alex, I need you to tell me everything you can about this kid," I said. "Who is he? What's his name? How did you meet him?"

"Uh– His name is Ian. I met him on a forum a month ago."

"You were there to talk about Emma?"

"Yeah." He was already out of breath. "And Ian understood me. He went through the same thing."

"Does he go to this school?"

"No," he said. "He's older. 24 I think."

"And he wanted to help you plan this?"

"It was his idea," said Alex. "He said it would make everything right."

It explained so much... Alex's rapid descent into darkness last month. The sudden calm. And the ancient graphing calculator, which students never used anymore. I had to admit, it was a clever way to communicate without leaving a technical trace.

"Alex, I need you to tell me the truth." I tried to catch my breath. "Do you really want to help stop this, or are you still messing with me?"

He didn't answer immediately. "I guess I want to help."

That wasn't convincing.

I got the sense that Alex didn't even know what he wanted to do yet. And that scared the hell out of me.

"Because all the stuff I said in my office, it's true. You can feel better. I promise." Then I added, "You know Ian's exploiting you, right? He's just using you to play out his own fantasies."

I felt like a lawyer, trying to make my case, to convince the jury to take my side.

Alex nodded, and that was it. Our sixty seconds were up.

We turned the corner and slowed down in front of the library doors. I peered through the glass and saw a group of students huddled by the reference desk. Ian towered over them, pointing his gun.

"Walk me in there, and keep the gun at my head," I whispered. "Tell him you want me to watch them die, so I can see what a failure I am."

"What the fuck is wrong with you?" Alex whispered back.

"Just do it," I hissed. Then I pushed open the doors and we walked inside.

Ian quickly turned his gun to us.

"Why's the shrink here?"

"To fuck with our heads," said Alex, lowering his gun. "Like I said on the phone, don't listen to a goddamn word the snake says. Now give me something loaded."

What the hell, Alex?

Alex and Ian gave each other big smiles, then walked toward one another and embraced.

"The Glock 19, right?"

"Yeah."

Ian handed Alex the gun and turned his attention back to the group of students. I quickly scanned the group, and that's when I saw Emma.

My heart sank. Why was she here? I called her father last night to warn him. Who would send their kid to school after that? He, of all people, should have known better.

It was easy to see why Alex fell for Emma. She was beautiful, but in more of an innocent, unassuming kind of way. She cowered with the other students, tears streaming down her cheeks.

"The cops are going to be here any minute," said Alex. "Let's do this."

The students whimpered. Emma let out a loud sob.

"Shut up, bitch!" Ian shouted.

She cried again and buried her face in her hands.

For just a second, Alex actually looked upset.

And that's when I realized that Emma being here was actually a *good* thing. I wasn't the one who needed to manipulate anyone.

"Alex, she needs you," I said gently.

He spun around and pointed the gun at me. "Enough out of you. You're going to watch us kill every single one of them. Maybe that'll finally shut that fucking mouth up."

"Look at her," I continued. "She's in distress, and you're the only one who can save her."

He lunged forward and hit me in the face with his gun.

"Shut. The. Fuck. Up."

But even from the ground, I persisted. "You can save her, Alex. You can be her hero."

I looked at Emma and raised my eyebrows, trying to imply that she should play along with me.

She gave me a pained look and closed her eyes.

"Please save me, Alex."

Yes.

Finally, I saw it. The softening of Alex's face. Just like in my office before.

"Dude, just kill the whore," said Ian. "Don't you remember what she did to you?"

"Please save me, Alex," repeated Emma through tears. "I need you."

"Are you fucking kidding me with this shit?" Ian laughed and pointed his gun at Emma. "Here, I'll get us started."

Emma screamed.

Then there was a gunshot.

And before I could piece together what happened, Ian was laying on the ground next to me, a pool of blood forming around his head.

I looked up and saw Alex standing over us, white as a sheet.

"You did it," I whispered. "You did it, Alex. You saved her."

His eyes brimmed with tears, but I knew he wouldn't cry.

"Alex, you're her hero. You rescued Emma."

His face stayed soft, exactly the state we needed to keep him in until the police got here.

I knew I'd be in huge trouble, but in my book, one dead murderer was better than twelve innocent students.

Call it reckless if you want, but as the sirens closed in around us, I knew I'd sleep soundly tonight.

If it wasn't for that next fucking gunshot.

Before I knew it, Alex had fallen on top of me, and I felt something warm spilling all over my chest.

"What the—"

I looked up and saw Emma standing above us.

"He's not my fucking savior!" she screamed.

"Emma, I need you to calm—"

"He's a stalker and a psycho!" she sobbed. "He made me afraid to come to school."

"I understand," I said, still on the ground with Alex bleeding out on top of me. "Can you drop the gun, so we can make sure no one else gets hurt?"

"I'm not dropping it." She shook her head. "When you called last night, my dad gave me his gun and told me to use it if anything happened. You should have stopped this. You shouldn't have used me like a pawn. I don't trust you. I don't trust anyone."

Her dad was in the military. He must have taken the threat seriously after all.

"You're safe now, Emma," I said calmly. "I promise."

She wiped her eyes. "I don't even know what 'safe' feels like anymore."

"I just want to make sure the police don't hurt you when they see a gun in your hands," I said. "Can you slide it over to the other side of the library?"

She sniffled and considered it for a few seconds. She finally nodded and pushed the gun away.

I let out a deep breath as the police burst through the doors.

There was shouting and crying, but I didn't pay much attention.

Instead, I looked into Alex's eyes, which were mere inches from my face. I saw sadness, but I also saw pride. I saw the face of a young man who felt he had redeemed himself.

I ran my hand through his hair and whispered, "I'm sorry."

So, you see, the truth is complicated.

Reckless? Probably. But I'm convinced that phone call saved twelve lives, even if it cost the life of my patient.

Maybe you think I should have just let the hostage negotiators do their jobs. I guess we'll never know.

Maybe you think I was being manipulative and controlling, but I only do that stuff because I don't believe people can be trusted to do the right thing.

Maybe you think this will scare me away from therapy forever, but I've seen it all... A patient with OCD whose loved ones really *did* suffer every time he missed a ritual. A choir boy who claimed he was being molested – not by a priest – but by God Himself. A patient with PTSD who gave *me* nightmares. A husband and wife who accused each other of abuse, and only one of them was telling the truth. A woman who kept her ex locked up as a sex slave. A pedo-ring conspiracy theorist who was actually onto something.

And how could I ever forget, Patient #220.

The problem is, my patients have a habit of dying. Alex isn't the first, and I'm worried he won't be the last. Sometimes I wonder if I'm the common denominator. Or maybe that's just the cost of taking on exceptionally broken clients.

I picked up my crate of belongings and took one last look around the office. I would miss this place and the people, but I would find another home soon enough.

I'll never stop trying to help.

End of Patient File #107

A Note on Emma

You might wonder if Emma was charged for killing Alex.

Yes, she was.

I actually testified at her trial, but there is very little value to the opinion of a therapist who never treated her.

But I could talk about Alex.

Yes, he was showing signs of a possible recovery. But that didn't erase his behavior from the months prior.

Alex had stalked her and repeatedly violated her boundaries. He ranted about her to anyone who would listen. In the trial, there was evidence of a relentless cyber-harassment campaign as well. He eventually held a gun to her head, and she believed her life was about to end.

Because of that, I agreed with the defense that Emma could very well have PTSD.

Have you ever had someone frantically obsessed with you? Someone who keeps contacting you, despite your repeated attempts to end that contact? Someone angry and unpredictable, someone who refuses to back down?

You fear for your life every second of the day. You don't sleep anymore. You have nightmares constantly, as your body tries to keep you alert. The primal fear instincts kick in, and they don't easily shut down.

Alex may have redeemed himself in his own eyes, but the fact is, he prevented a situation *he created.*

OCD Rituals

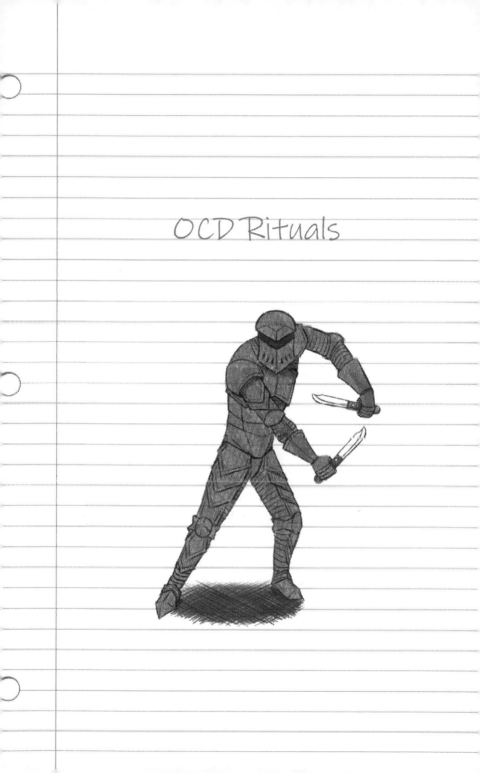

OCD Rituals

PART ONE

"Love one. Love two…"

As he spoke, Phil held his hand to his heart and raised one finger, then two. Then he bowed his head and whispered one last sentence:

"Sorry for bothering you."

In my notebook, I finished sketching that pointy S symbol that we all drew in high school. I never actually write anything down, but it gives patients the comforting idea that I'm in the process of "figuring it out".

"How often do you perform this ritual, Phil?" I asked.

He looked up. "Every five minutes."

He had a messy beard and a weathered face that made him appear much older than he probably was.

"Five minutes?" I repeated, trying not to sound too surprised. That was unusually frequent, even for a patient with severe OCD. "Do you feel any relief after the ritual is complete?"

He shook his head. "Never."

"What are you afraid will happen if you don't perform the ritual?"

He closed his eyes and shook his head.

"Phil, you can tell me," I said encouragingly. "That's what I'm here for."

He took a deep breath. "The– The man with two knives."

Fear of death or murder was one of the most common manifestations of OCD. But of course, I didn't want to minimize his fear, which was still very real to him.

"That sounds frightening, Phil," I said. "Can you tell me more about this man?"

He swallowed. "If I miss a ritual, he comes in the middle of the night. And he– he –"

"It's okay," I said gently. "I don't want to upset you."

I turned to his wife, who was anxiously massaging his knee with her hand.

"Anne, how has this impacted you?" I asked. "It must be difficult, seeing your husband suffer this way. You must worry every day, especially when he's at work or traveling?"

"He never leaves the house," she said quietly. "This is the first time he's been out in three years. He's been on disability the whole time. He's so terrified. And–"

My new assistant, Noah, opened the door.

"Noah, I'm in the middle of a session."

"Sorry, it's the school." He blushed. "They said it's urgent. They want to talk about Emma's trial."

I shook my head and apologized.

"I'll be right back."

As I walked out of the office, Noah stood in the doorway and stared at Phil and Anne. Apparently he learned nothing from orientation. But I didn't have time to deal with him right now.

I stepped out and took the call. The school wanted me to testify in Emma's favor, which I was already planning to do. I got the sense they were more worried I would try to blame the school, as revenge for firing me.

But revenge is petty, especially at the cost of a young person's future.

I finished the call and returned to my office.

"I'm so sorry for the interruption," I said as I took my seat. "Now, there's good news and bad news here. The bad news is that you certainly seem to be suffering from a severe case of Obsessive Compulsive Disorder. The good news is that you came in for help, and OCD is very treatable."

Phil leaned forward. "You can stop him?"

"Yes," I said confidently. "I'm not a huge fan of medication, but I think antidepressants could help take the edge off while we begin a regimen of mindfulness and talk therapy. In a few months, those rituals will be a thing of the past. My whole team is here to help you."

I didn't want to refer him out to my colleagues too quickly, but this was a pretty classic case of OCD, and I felt that my resources might be better spent on patients with more unusual issues.

Phil shook his head. "No."

"I'm sorry?"

"No, I can't take medications. I can't stop the rituals."

"Of course you can," I said. "That's why we're here."

"No," he said again. "Otherwise he'll do it again."

I was becoming a bit frustrated by this point. "Phil, that's the whole reason—"

"Show us," Phil said to his wife.

She winced and shook her head slightly.

"Please," Phil pleaded. "Show us."

Anne closed her eyes and lifted up her shirt.

Her torso was covered in at least a dozen stab wounds.

Before I even had a chance to react, Phil held his hand to his heart again.

"Love one. Love two..."

Jesus Christ. Had it already been five minutes?

"Sorry for bothering you."

PART TWO

I poked my head out the office door.

"Noah, what's my afternoon look like?"

He took out the iPad.

"Uhh… Two new patients after this one," he said. "Don Halverson–"

"Noah, we've been over this," I said impatiently. "I can't remember names. I remember *problems*. Read from Column B, please."

"Oh, right," he said, scanning the screen. "Uh– Guy who intentionally transmitted HIV to eight people."

"And the other one?"

"Homeless kid who escaped a cult."

As the words came out of his mouth he raised his eyebrows. "Jeez, doc…"

"Welcome to the wonderful world of pro-bono work, Noah." I gave him a quick smile. "Please move them to next week. I'm going to need a little extra time with my current patients."

They both sounded fascinating, but the homeless kid was probably hallucinating from drugs, and the HIV guy was court-ordered, so he wouldn't be hurting more people any time soon. Right now, Phil needed my full attention.

I returned to my office and saw Phil and Anne embracing each other. They must have been the most exhausted-looking couple I've ever worked with.

"Anne," I began gently. "Now that I've seen evidence of bodily harm, I have to report this to the police. Do you understand?"

"No!" They both shouted at the same time.

"It's not really a matter of choice—"

"You can't," said Anne. "That's the whole reason we're here. If we go to the police, he'll kill Phil."

I tilted my head. "How can you possibly know that?"

"Because of Eleanor," Phil answered for her.

"Eleanor?"

"Our daughter," said Phil quietly. "She had the same— the same condition as me."

"OCD?"

"It's not OCD!" he protested. "Eleanor went to the police last month, and the man with two knives—"

Anne held his hand.

"He killed her, a week after the police detail left our house," Phil stammered. "The angriest we've ever seen him. Stabbed her eight times and dragged her into the woods."

What the hell had I gotten myself into here?

"Let's take a step back here," I said. "Phil, do you have any recollection of when this ritual began?"

"Three years ago," he said. "We took Eleanor on a trip to Disney, and all we remember is waking up and hearing him tell Eleanor and I that we had to do the ritual every day – from 4am to 11pm – or he would hurt our family. There were 3 rules: No cops, no hospitals, and no skipping sleep. We thought it was some kind of sick joke at first, so we didn't do the rituals, but then he showed up that night…"

"Do you have any idea what the ritual means?" I asked. "Love one, Love two, any of that?"

He nodded.

"She's Love One." He pointed to Anne. "Her sister is Love Two. If I miss either of them, they get punished that night."

"Wait, her sister gets stabbed too?"

"Yes," Anne whispered. "She lives with us. And she has two more scars than me."

"How many do you have?" I asked.

"14."

Phil bowed his head in shame. But by my calculations, he

was nothing short of a hero.

12 rituals every hour, 19 hours per day, 365 days per year, for 3 years.

249,660 rituals. And he only missed 14 times.

That's a 99.995% success rate.

"What about 'sorry for bothering you'?" I asked. "What does that part mean?"

He shook his head. "I have no idea."

We sat there in silence for a while, and I just stared at my notebook in disbelief.

Then Phil spoke up again.

"You have to help us," he begged. "We've tried everything, but he's always watching. I don't think he's human. I think– I think he might be a demon or a ghost."

I did my best to conceal a *harumph*. Yeah, I don't believe in that stuff. To me, those are code-words for "overactive amygdala", which was – unsurprisingly – another aspect of OCD. I like to think every mystery has a practical explanation, set here on planet Earth.

"So your daughter – Eleanor – she had to do the same ritual, or the same thing would happen?"

They nodded.

There was no point in pretending to write in my notebook anymore. I had no idea what was happening.

Father, mother, sister, daughter. Father and daughter have to perform 5-minute rituals otherwise mother and sister get stabbed by omniscient stalker.

I didn't know what was worse. The fact that they refused to involve the police because of this omniscient stalker, or the fact that I was about to go along with it.

"Phil, I need to be honest with you," I said. "Given the severity of your OCD, I have suspicions that you may also be suffering from co-morbid episodes of dissociation."

"Dissociation?"

"When we disconnect from our bodies and minds," I said. "It's possible that you could be the man with two knives, *and* his victim."

"My god, will you stop diagnosing people with mental disorders and *listen* to us?" Anne spoke up angrily. "We have surveillance videos, we wired the whole house. It's not Phil. It's some sort of... evil spirit."

"You have videos?" I asked, curious. "May I view them?" Hopefully we could put an end to this supernatural talk, once and for all.

She nodded and took out her phone.

"This is from last year," she said, handing the phone to me. "Phil accidentally said 'Love You' instead of 'Love Two'."

I watched the footage – four panels at once. In the master bedroom, Phil and Anne made their way into their bed. In the guest room, Anne's sister read a book in bed before shutting off the lights. In Eleanor's room, a young teen girl typed away on her laptop before finally drifting off to sleep. The front entrance to the house showed no signs of life.

Then I just waited. Phil did his ritual a few times on the couch while I continued watching.

But nothing happened for a long time. I wasn't sure if I was missing something.

And that's when I saw it.

A man in full body armor marched into the sister's bedroom. He had two butcher's knives, one in each hand.

I'm normally not a sucker for horror, but I'll admit I jumped. I wanted to call out and warn her.

And then, with surgical precision, he lifted one knife and drove it into her stomach.

She lurched out of bed and screamed, and just like that, the man with two knives walked out of the frame. The others bolted out of bed and ran for her room, but I was busy watching the front door.

No one ever came out.

Jesus Christ. That video changed everything. I've been wrong plenty of times, but I've never been *this* wrong. Could Phil even be diagnosed with OCD if his fears were completely rational?

I handed the phone back to Anne and said, "This is

terrifying. I'm so sorry for—"

"*Love one, love two…*" Phil began his ritual again. "*Sorry for bothering you.*"

For some reason, that last sentence really made me uncomfortable. Something about the way Phil whispered it in that lower voice – it didn't even sound like him.

He pressed a button on his Apple Watch and looked back up to us.

"Is that how you keep track of the 5-minute intervals?"

He nodded. "It vibrates 30 seconds before. Then loud alarm at 20 seconds. And at 10 seconds, it calls everyone."

I shook my head. What kind of life was this?

"I'm so sorry for doubting you," I said. "This must be hell for you and your family."

"We have the video of Eleanor too," said Anne through tears. "The one where he took her away from us."

I bit my lip and accepted the phone.

For the next few minutes, I watched their family perform their nighttime routine again. And then later in the night, the man appeared again. This time, he walked into Eleanor's room and covered her mouth. She squirmed violently, but no one in the house could hear her. Then he began stabbing her repeatedly – almost as if he was punishing her. Eventually, her body went limp, and he dragged her body downstairs and out the front door.

I closed the phone and shoved it back to Anne, as if it had some kind of curse that could be passed along to me. *What had gotten into me?*

"You've searched the house for him, right?" I asked. "Because he doesn't seem to enter or exit the house."

"Of course we have," said Phil. "I'm telling you, he's not human."

I cleared my throat. "I fully understand your conclusions, but I'm a student of science," I said. "Would it be okay if we tried my way – the scientific method? Just a few controlled experiments. And if that doesn't work, you're free to explore a medium or ghost hunter."

"Experiments?" Phil asked nervously.

"I would like access to your security feed," I said. "I think he has access too, hence why he's able to watch your every ritual. So I want to be in a contained room with you, while we try various combinations of your ritual. If this man doesn't know whether or not you perform the ritual–"

"He always knows!" Phil protested. "He'll hurt them."

Anne squeezed his hand tighter. "We'll do it."

"What?"

"Please, Phil," she said. "We have to try something. I can't live like this anymore."

He took a deep breath and nodded.

"So what do you need us to do?"

"Phil, I'd like you to stay with me in this office for the next couple of days. I'll get some blankets for the couch," I said. "Anne, I need you and your sister to act like everything is normal at home, even in Phil's absence. And if you suspect anything is off, please call me."

They both nodded apprehensively.

After answering a few more of their questions, I escorted Anne from my office.

"Noah, can you stay late these next few nights? I'll pay you overtime."

I needed someone to watch the door and make sure no one was listening.

"Sure thing, Dr. Harpy."

I stared at him. "Harp-*er*," I said. "Harpy is a rude, foul-tempered woman."

He went pink. "Oh, right."

Experiment #1: Control Group - Do The Ritual

First, I had to set a baseline. What happened if Phil did the ritual successfully every 5 minutes in my office, with only me watching, and no one else?

29

So that's what we did for the rest of the afternoon and evening. I just sat across from Phil and watched him perform his ritual every 5 minutes.

He did it with such a sense of duty and purpose. It was somehow both disturbing and inspiring to witness.

Finally, we reached 11pm and I turned to the security camera feed on my laptop. Anne and her sister made their way into bed, and for the rest of the night, nothing happened.

A lucky guess for the man with two knives.

Tomorrow we would make things more interesting.

Experiment #2: Experimental Group - Forget Love One

"Today, I need you to mess up 'Love One'."

Phil looked at me miserably. "Please…"

"He won't hurt Anne," I said encouragingly. "There's no possible way he'll know you missed, let alone *who* you missed. It's just the two of us in this room."

He took a deep breath and nodded.

But for the next eight rituals, he continued to say everything correctly.

"Phil, I promise everyone is going to be okay," I said. "Don't you want to save Anne from this hell?"

He looked up to me and closed his eyes. "Okay."

We waited another five minutes for his Apple Watch to light up, and then I leaned forward in anticipation.

"*Love— Three— Love Two. Sorry for bothering you.*"

He fell back into the couch and burst into tears.

"Oh god," he said. "I've doomed her again."

I rushed over and comforted him. "You're helping her," I said. "So you don't have to live like this anymore."

He continued the rituals correctly for the rest of the day and evening. Then I turned back to the security feed and watched Anne and her sister perform their nighttime routine. Phil refused to watch.

They fell asleep and nothing happened. *I knew it.* The man wasn't omniscient. He was just watching their security feed.

But then, out of the corner of my eye, I saw something change in Anne's video.

It was him.

How the hell—

I lunged for my phone and called Anne's cell phone. She didn't answer.

"Fuck," I whispered.

"What's happening?" Phil asked.

"Call Anne's sister!" I said. "Do it now!"

I watched the video as the man walked robotically toward Anne in bed.

"He's there," I heard Phil speak into his phone. "He's going for Anne."

He ended the call without another word.

"Why did you hang up!"

"There's no point," said Phil, defeated. "He can't be stopped."

Heart racing, I turned back to the video feed as the man walked closer.

"Wake up, Anne..." I stared at the screen and bit my lips. "Get out of there."

And then I watched as the man drove the knife into Anne's thigh.

"What the FUCK!" I kicked my trash bin across the room. "How did he know?"

"We keep trying to tell you... He's not human," said Phil.

I shook my head and stormed out of the room.

"Noah!" I barked. "When I took that phone call with the school yesterday, did anyone come in or out of my office?"

"No, doc." He shook his head, eyes wide. He'd never seen me like this before.

"How did he know?" I repeated under my breath as I turned back toward my office.

Then Noah spoke up again. "Maybe he really *is* a demon?"

I spun around. "Are you— Are you listening to our sessions?"

He went white. "Uh– Only a little."

"Noah…" I rubbed my fingers into my eyes. "You need to go home."

"Come on!" he said. "I'm– I'm experienced with psychology stuff."

"You took Psych 101 in college!" I said, exasperated. "I don't have time for this."

"What if he's really a demon though?" said Noah. "Shouldn't you–"

"He's not a demon!" I snapped, turning back to my office. "Someone is *listening* to us."

And that's when it hit me like a ton of bricks.

Oh my god.

I hurried back into the office and approached Phil.

"Phil, I'm so sorry for failing you," I said. "I need to get us some dinner. I'll be right back."

Before he could respond, I held my index finger up to his lips, and reached down for his Apple Watch. I unfastened the metal strap and carefully removed it from his wrist, placing it on the table without making a sound.

I took my finger from his lips and motioned for him to follow me out of the office.

He did.

"What's going on?" he whispered when we got into the lobby.

"I think someone is listening through your watch," I said quietly. "You wear it wherever you go, right?"

"Yes." He nodded. "All day, every day."

"Ohhh…" Noah nodded gravely from behind his desk.

I gave him a light smack on the head with my notebook. "*Not a demon.*"

"But who would be listening?" asked Phil.

"I don't know," I said. "But we've bought ourselves some time. He thinks you're alone in my office, and you don't need to perform your ritual until morning, which gives us about three hours to figure out who's doing this to you."

"But how?" asked Phil. "How can we figure it out?"

"I've spent all this time playing detective, I've forgotten to do my actual job," I said. "Phil, I need to know about your past."

"What do you mean?" he asked.

"Before the ritual," I said. "Who were you? What was your life like? Any enemies... bitter exes, bad business deals?"

"Or loans from the mafia..." Noah said seriously.

I glared at him.

"I don't remember." Phil shook his head. "I can't remember anything from before the Disney trip. We woke up in a daze. It felt like we'd been drugged."

"You don't remember anything about your life before that?"

He shook his head.

I thought for a moment, and then said, "Have you ever been hypnotized?"

He raised his eyebrows. "Like where magicians make you do funny stuff?"

"No, that's stage hypnosis," I said. "In therapy, we use it to calm the patient and access a deeper state of mind. You still have full control of your mind and body. Some call it pseudo-science, but I've seen several patients uncover forgotten memories with it."

"I'll try anything."

"Great," I said. "This isn't exactly an ideal environment, but we don't have the luxury of time, so we'll have to make do. Noah, can you dim the lights?"

He eagerly jumped out of his seat and turned down the lights. Then he sat back down at his desk.

I looked at him and pointed to the building's front door. "Out."

"Oh, come on— let me stay!" he said. "I won't cause any trouble."

"Noah—"

"It's fine." Phil spoke up softly. "I don't mind."

Noah gave him a huge smile. I rolled my eyes and turned back to Phil.

We sat down in the waiting room chairs and I began the hypnotic induction. You don't do it with a swinging necklace, like in the movies. Normally I'd approach it with a gradual relaxation method, but we only had a few hours before Phil had to start his rituals again, so the rapid Elman method was probably our best bet.

"I want you to close your eyes, and then imagine your eyes are too tired to stay open…" I said quietly. "Like when you've had a long few days with no sleep, and your head finally hits a pillow… Finally, you can let go and catch up on your rest… Your dreams get started very quickly… The harder you try to open your eyes, the harder they stay shut…"

He closed his eyes, and we continued down this path for a few minutes.

"Now, when I drop your left hand into your lap, you will go ten times deeper…" I gently lifted his left hand, then lowered it slowly and placed it on his leg. He rocked slightly from side to side.

We did the same with his right hand, and then got started on counting clouds. "As each cloud blows away with the breeze, you fall into a deeper state… Deeper and deeper every time…"

After a few more minutes, I felt confident that Phil had entered a hypnotic state. That was lucky. A lot of people don't respond to it, because their logical mind is too busy trying to prove it wrong.

I'm one of those people.

"Now, Phil," I spoke in a calming voice. "What can you tell me about your childhood?"

He took a relaxing breath. "I don't remember."

"That's okay," I said. "What about your trip to Disney with your daughter, Eleanor?"

His face broke into a sad smile. "I loved Eleanor."

"She sounded like a very special person," I said. "What was her favorite ride at Disney?"

He swayed a bit. "I don't remember."

This was unusual for hypnosis. Usually patients were more receptive to questions.

"What about your ritual?" I asked. "Do you have any idea what 'sorry for bothering you' means?"

He shook his head slowly. "I don't know."

"Could you try performing the ritual for us now, Phil?"

He nodded. *"Love one, Love Two... Sorry for bothering you."*

His voice got deep and raspy with that last sentence again.

"Can you do it again?"

"Love one, Love Two... Sorry for bothering you."

"Just the last part now?"

"Sorry for bothering you." He repeated it in that same low voice.

"Again?"

"Sorry for bothering you."

"Again?"

"Sorry for bothering you," he said. *"But can you spare some change for a vet and his little girl?"*

He held his hand out to me.

I stared at it for a moment. Vet and his little girl...? Spare change...?

Did Phil used to be homeless or something?

And then my heart started racing.

Holy shit.

"Noah," I whispered. "That new patient I asked you to push back yesterday..."

He frowned. "The dude who gave people HIV?"

"No," I said, "That homeless kid– the one who claimed to escape from a cult. What was that patient's name?"

He took out his iPad and started swiping hurriedly.

"Homeless kid who escaped a cult," he said.

I stared at him incredulously. "The name, Noah!" I said. "Column A."

He swiped one more time and then his face froze, illuminated by the light of the iPad.

"Woah..."

"For god's sake, what's the name!"

"Eleanor," he whispered. "Her name is Eleanor."

PART THREE

I don't want to lose your respect, but you're about to see a different side of me.

One thing you need to understand about me is that I *despise* psychological torture. At least with physical torture, the victim knows the perpetrator is causing their suffering.

But with psychological torture, the perpetrator plays innocent while the victim self-destructs and blames themselves.

Do it to a homeless veteran and his family, and unfortunately you've incurred my deepest disgust.

You're already aware that I have a bit of a temper, but today is going to be different.

I am a flawed person, just like any other, with secrets and regrets.

Today, you will learn one of those secrets.

But I wouldn't quite call it a regret.

"Eleanor?" Phil stood up from his chair. "Did you say Eleanor?"

"Phil, I think your daughter might still be alive." I reached out and touched his shoulder. "I think she might have come to this very office."

His eyes welled with tears. "Alive?"

"I can't say for certain," I said. "But it would explain a lot. She has the same name as your daughter, and you both have some sort of history with homelessness. She also claims she escaped from a cult – and you're showing some pretty severe signs of brainwashing."

"Brainwashing?"

"Up until a moment ago, you weren't able to remember most of your life," I said. "For the past three years, you've been deprived of sleep and forced into this terrifying, life-consuming ritual. It would be enough to make anyone lose their mind."

"Where is Eleanor now?" asked Phil. He didn't seem to care about his own suffering at all. He just wanted to know about his daughter.

"Noah, I know it's late, but can you try to reach Eleanor at the number listed in her file?" I asked. "We only have one hour before Phil needs to start his rituals again, and she may already have the answers we need."

He nodded. "You got it, boss."

"The rituals," said Phil miserably. "Do I have to keep doing them?"

"I don't know," I said truthfully. "We still don't know who the man with two knives is. If you don't resume the ritual, I think he'll keep harming them."

Phil looked to the ground.

"It won't be for long," I reassured him. "We're going to figure this out."

"I just don't understand," he said. "Who would want to do this to us?"

"I don't know," I said. I found myself saying that a lot with Phil.

"I just want to see my daughter again."

"Phil, can you remember anything else from the hypnosis?" I asked. "Anything at all?"

He shook his head. "Sorry."

"I can get you back into that state, but we're running out of time until you have to start the ritual," I said. "It would be best if we could just get ahold of Eleanor. Do you have any idea where she might be staying? Any past shelters or friends?"

He closed his eyes tight and waited for a few seconds. Then he sighed and looked up. "I'm sorry, I can't remember."

I turned to Noah. "What about you? Any luck?"

"No, doc," he said. "I've tried five times. She's not answering."

"Let me give it a try from my cell." I walked over to the desk. "Maybe she'll recognize my number from her initial call."

"Don't worry about it," he said gently. "I've got it, doc. You've gotta take care of Phil."

"Thanks." I nodded and walked back to Phil. "Do you want to try the hypnosis again?"

"Sure," he said. "Whatever you think will help."

For the next fifteen minutes, we attempted the same induction method, but it didn't seem to be working anymore. Phil kept opening his eyes, and he didn't seem relaxed like before.

"Is everything okay?" I asked. "You don't seem quite as receptive to my suggestions."

"I'm sorry," he said. "I can't stop thinking about Eleanor. It has me so distracted."

"No, don't blame yourself." It was silly to think he could enter a hypnotic state after learning that his daughter was actually alive. We'd just wasted precious time, and now we only had 45 minutes until the rituals started again.

Maybe we couldn't get Phil back into the hypnotic state, but there were other clues to this mystery. I sat down and reviewed the security footage over and over again. I watched him stab Anne until I couldn't stand to watch it anymore.

Who was this guy? Fully body armor, gas mask... It was the stuff of nightmares.

Out of ideas, I turned to Noah. "Still nothing?"

He jolted up from his desk. "What– Oh, uh– No, sorry."

"Were you *sleeping*?" I stormed over to the desk. "Give me the phone."

"No, I got it!"

But I snatched the phone and Eleanor's file from his hands and dialed the number.

"Hello?" A girl's voice answered after two rings.

My heart jumped. "Eleanor?"

"Yes..." she said. "Who is this? It's the middle of the night."

"Eleanor, this is Dr. Harper," I said. "You had an appointment with me two days ago–"

"And you canceled it at the last second."

"Yes," I said. "Because I was treating your father, Phil."

There was a long pause on the other end.

"He's– He's one of your patients?"

"Yes," I said. "And we need your help. I don't have time to explain– we need you in the office now."

"My dad is there with you?"

"That's right," I said. "Please, can you come?"

"Yes," she said. "It's a ten minute cab ride. I'll leave now."

"Thank you so much," I said. "And I'm sorry about all of the late-night calls."

"What do you mean?"

"Well, we've been ringing you for the past hour."

There was another pause. "I don't have any missed calls from you. This was the first."

I felt my stomach drop, but I tried to keep acting normal. "Okay, see you soon."

I hung up the phone and – without thinking – I lunged at Noah.

"Who are you!"

"Woah, what?"

I pushed him against the wall. "Brand new assistant, listening in on my sessions, delaying us at every step with your bumbling incompetence... Who are you!"

"What are you talking about, doc?"

I pushed harder, hands closing in around his neck.

"I've had bad assistants before," I growled. "But nobody is *this* fucking stupid."

He started choking, tugging away at my grip.

I punched him in the face and he fell to the ground.

Phil rushed over. "What did you do that for?"

"He was lying," I said. "He wasn't calling Eleanor."

"Why would he lie about that?"

"I don't know," I said. "But we'll find out when he wakes up. Here, help me tie him up."

Phil bent down with me and we secured Noah to the desk with my belt.

My own assistant. How could I have been so blind? He had access the entire time, and I just kept giving him more.

I was supposed to be good at reading people.

Eleanor arrived ten minutes later, exactly as promised.

The moment she opened the door, Phil sprinted toward her and pulled her into the longest hug I've ever seen. I couldn't even tell if they were crying or laughing. Maybe a bit of both.

"I don't want to interrupt," I said. "But we only have 30 minutes until the rituals start up again."

They broke their embrace and turned to me. Eleanor had a soft kindness in her eyes, just like her father. She had to be about sixteen by this point, but she carried none of the innocence someone her age should have.

"Eleanor, how— how did you escape?"

"After the stabbing, I pretended to be dead," she said. "They dragged me into the woods and went back to the house for a shovel to bury me. That's when I ran."

Phil pulled her closer. "I'm so proud of you."

"You said it's a cult?" I asked. "What kind of cult?"

"It's called *My Happy Family*," she said. "It's more like a lot of little cults. They call themselves hobbyists. I found their forum on the dark web. They share brainwashing techniques – for forcing people into your family."

I raised my eyebrows. "Forcing people into your family?"

"Yeah, like with dad and me, that ritual wasn't unique," she said. "People have been perfecting it for years and reporting back with their experiences. Apparently they used to punish the person who missed the ritual, but that sometimes made them suicidal, and you don't want your investment to commit suicide."

"Investment?"

"Yeah, that's what they call the people they're brainwashing," she said. "They put a ton of time and emotional energy into their investments, so they want to make sure you stay a long time."

"So they switched to hurting other family members?"

"Right," said Eleanor. "If you're afraid for your own life, you might eventually give up. But if you're afraid of hurting someone you love, you'll keep doing the ritual forever."

"That's sick."

"Yeah, they use a lot of CIA mind-control techniques," she said. "And then they chart their results to determine the best methods. It's all just based around votes and most popular comments. For example, one poll determined that five hours of sleep is just enough to maintain docility without causing too much exhaustion. So now everyone goes with five hours. They're like a hive mind."

"But how can someone just forget who they were and join a new family?"

"Well, they tend to go after vulnerable populations," she said. "Homeless people, drug addicts, prostitutes... They offer something nice, like an Apple Watch, and then they load you up with benzos."

"Like Xanax?"

"Right," she said. "After a few weeks, your memory turns to mush. Then they start up the rituals and replace your memories with new ones. It's only a matter of time before you accept your new reality."

"And people just forget their old life?"

"That's why they do the ritual in such frequent intervals," she said. "That way you spend every moment of your life thinking about the ritual, paralyzed by the fear of what happens if you miss it. Constant fear messes with the rest of your brain."

I couldn't argue with her there. She could have quite a future in this career someday.

I took a deep breath. "Eleanor, is this the man with two knives?"

I walked over to the desk and pointed at Noah.

She took one look at Noah and frowned.

"There is no man," she said. "That's what I'm trying to say.

It's just them."

"Just who?" asked Phil.

"Wait…" She looked at Phil. "You don't know about Anne yet?"

I raised my eyebrows. It was strange to hear a girl refer to her mother by name.

"You're saying your mom is involved in all this?"

"She's not my mom," said Eleanor. "She and Rose are the whole operation."

"What?" I frowned. "So you and your dad–"

Phil spoke weakly. "We're their investment."

I shook my head, trying to absorb what Eleanor was telling us.

"It's not possible. I've seen the security videos."

She let out a cold laugh. "Yeah, that's one of their favorite methods," she said. "They call it *digital hallucination*. Almost all of them have it set up, because it erases any doubts the investment might have. Here, show me one of your videos."

I took out my cell phone and played the most recent attack.

"There! See?" She pointed to Rose's room before the man even arrived.

"What am I supposed to be seeing?"

"The book," she said. "*Great Expectations*. Every single night Anne gets attacked, Rose is reading that book before bedtime. Here, look."

She took out her phone and scrolled through to find a video. I watched with morbid fascination as Rose opened *Great Expectations* and eventually turned out the lights.

"The timestamps are the same *every time*," said Eleanor. "It's a loop. And whenever Rose gets stabbed, Anne and dad's video always shows the same thing too. On the forum, they all help each other doctor the clips."

"Wait a minute," I said in disbelief. "Phil, right before Anne got attacked earlier, I asked you to call Rose – she answered, right?"

"Yes." He nodded.

"What time was that?"

He took out his phone and scrolled through his calls. "12:47am"

I skipped the security video to 12:46am and watched intently. One minute passed as the man with two knives entered Anne's room. Rose remained fast asleep in her room. Then 12:47 hit. Exactly when Phil talked with Rose.

But in the video, Rose remained fast asleep.

"*What the hell...*" I wondered out loud.

"So the man with two knives—"

"Isn't a man at all," said Eleanor. "It's both of them. They just put on that creepy outfit, and then stab whoever got missed in the ritual."

"That's insane!" I said. "Why would they stab each other? Why not just stab another one of their other investments?"

"You know what codependency is, right?"

"Yes, of course. When one person feels an unhealthy emotional reliance on another – responsible for their wellbeing."

"And the rescuer mistakes that dependence for love, right?"

"Yes," I said. "So, let me get this straight. They make you feel guilty for hurting them, when they're the ones actually causing harm? And then they use that guilt to make you 'love' them? "

"That's why I made the appointment," said Eleanor. "I mean, I understand what happened to me, but I still can't get rid of the guilt. It's not like the scars from the knife. It's deep inside of me. Like a monster squeezing at my heart."

I felt my blood boiling. "They can't get away with this," I said. "Let's call the police now. We have everything we need to put them away."

Eleanor shook her head. "They all have detailed police plans," she said. "There's an entire subforum devoted to it. They get away with it almost every time, because it's their word against some brainwashed homeless person or drug addict."

"Can't the police get their IP addresses or something?" I said, growing increasingly agitated. "Did Anne and Rose ever post there?"

"Yes," said Eleanor. "That's how I found the forum in the first place. I saw it on Anne's computer the night I called the police. She left it open, and I recognized our whole Disney backstory in one of their posts."

"Perfect!" I said. "Can you show me the post? Then the police can find the IP."

She gave me a funny look. "There aren't any IPs," she said. "It's the dark web."

I gritted my teeth and repeated, "They can't get away with this."

"At least we're safe," said Phil, pulling Eleanor into a hug. "At least Eleanor is okay."

"But they're going to hurt someone else!" I said. "It's only a matter of time."

"Sorry, Dr. Harper." Eleanor shook her head. "I don't think there's any way we can stop it."

I thought for a moment and said, "What if we use their own tricks against them?"

"Phil, unfortunately I need to put you under 24/7 watch," I said. "I was wrong about the man with two knives, and now I can see your family is at serious risk."

"W– What?" Phil stammered. "You can't lock me up, my wife needs me."

"I just need to keep you for a little while," I said. "Until we can perform a few more experiments."

"No!" said Phil. "No more experiments. Please."

"There's something else at work here," I said. "I think you were right about the demon theory. But I have to figure it out – so your family can be at peace again."

"No!" said Phil. "We'll just go back to our rituals."

"Yes, the rituals start back up in a few minutes," I said. "I'm going to bind your hands and take you to the safe house now."

"Bind my– what?"

"That way you can't perform the ritual," I said. "So I can try a few more experiments."

"No!" Phil screamed. "You can't do that! You saw what he'll do to them!"

"I don't think he's going to hurt them anymore," I said. "Now, come on– let's go."

"No!" Phil sobbed. "No! You can't do this!"

He continued sobbing and shouting into the Apple Watch until we exited the office and returned to the lobby.

"That was good, Phil," I said quietly. "You could be an actor, you know."

"Thanks," he said. "So now... They'll think they still have control of their investment, and they'll wait for me – instead of taking someone else?"

"That's right," I said. "And I can keep monitoring them until we get enough evidence to send to the FBI. I really think we can get enough of a case here to open a major investigation."

"What about Anne and Rose?" asked Eleanor.

"I doubt they'll keep hurting each other," I said quickly. "Not if they know this could go on indefinitely."

"No, I mean they'll come into your office," said Eleanor. "They'll want to know where he is."

"Let me handle that," I said. "I'm quite good at telling people what they want to hear, as long as I know their motives. And thanks to you, now I do."

They both nodded.

"Phil, there's just one more question I have," I said. "Why did you come to me in the first place?"

"To therapy?"

"Yes."

He looked down, ashamed. "Anne suggested it, because I felt suicidal after Eleanor left," he said. "I thought it was because Anne cared about me, but apparently she just wanted to make sure her second *investment* didn't die."

Eleanor turned to me. "They probably thought they could trick you with their digital hallucinations too. That way you'd confirm their story, and dad would have no doubts left in his mind."

I bit my lip, hard.

I hated these people.

Suddenly there was a stirring from behind the desk.

"*Oh god*, Noah." I hurried over to him.

"W– What happened?" he asked in a daze.

"Nothing," I said quickly. "You just passed out."

He furrowed his brows and thought for a second. "You hit me."

I huffed.

"Yes, well," I said stiffly. " Be that as it may, we've determined you are no longer a threat."

He crossed his arms and glared at me.

"Uh– sorry to interrupt," said Phil. "But I think Eleanor and I are going to leave before it gets much later. The shelters tend to fill up fast."

"Oh no," I said. "Please, come stay with me for a while. The guest rooms are already made up. And you'll be so much safer there. I have quite an elaborate home security system."

That's what happens when you work with stalkers and the darker personality disorders.

"I don't know…" said Phil. "I don't want to impose."

"You're not imposing," I said. "I'd love to have you. You can sleep all day, and then I'll cook a big holiday dinner tonight. I make the best turnips you've ever had."

"Turnips?" Eleanor raised her eyebrows. "Blegh."

"Trust me." I smiled.

Phil and Eleanor looked at each other and did some sort of father-daughter communication with their eyes. Then Phil nodded. "We'd love to. Thank you."

Noah cleared his throat. His arms were still crossed.

"Oh, right," I said. "Noah, I'm sorry for punching you."

He continued glaring at me.

"… And I'm sorry for calling you stupid."

He didn't let up.

I sighed and rolled my eyes. "Noah, would you like to join

us for dinner tonight?"

Finally, he broke into a huge grin. "Awesome."

"Wait a minute…" I said. "Why *didn't* your calls go through to Eleanor?"

"I don't know!" he said. "I dialed it in, just like you taught me at orientation. With +661 at the beginning."

I sighed loudly and pressed my fingers into my eyes. "Five. Five."

"Huh?"

"It's +55, not 66." I let out a deep breath. "Jesus."

So, Noah wasn't a cult member after all. Just a cartoonishly oblivious assistant who took an inappropriate interest in my patients.

Honestly, I think I would have preferred cult-Noah.

People always assume my house is cold and dark, but it's actually quite cozy – especially around Christmas. I love the lights, decorations, all of it. It's a nice contrast from my otherwise bleak days.

We sat around the table as *Joy to the World* rang in the background. At our side, the tree twinkled with hundreds of gold ornaments and lights.

Joy to the world, Joy to the world! The Lord is come!

I closed my eyes and smiled. Good food, good music, and good people. If there was any purpose to life, this had to be it.

"You know," said Noah through a full mouth. "I had a feeling it was a cult."

Compared to the way Noah ate, you'd never guess Phil and Eleanor were the ones living on the street. He was already on his third plate.

And Heaven and nature sing!

"You thought it was a demon," I snapped.

"Yeah, but that was my third guess," he said. "Before that, it was mafia and cult."

"Whatever," I grumbled.

"Eleanor, please put your phone away at dinner," said Phil.

I looked over and saw her tapping away.

"Wait, check this out!" she said. "They posted on the forum again."

Joy to the World, the Savior reigns!

I leaned forward, curious to hear more. "Anne and Rose?"

"Yes," she said. "They posted about how dad got involuntarily committed, and how he's unable to perform his rituals. They asked if they should keep up the facade and continue hurting each other until he's released."

"Did anyone respond?" asked Phil.

"A bunch of people!" she said. "They're crazy… The top comment says it's better to get stabbed a few times now, than to start all over with a new investment, because new investments will mess up the ritual a few times anyways. Another says to keep at it, because the investment will probably ask to see the new wounds when he gets out. And then this guy wrote: *'Sounds like he still loves you. I would keep going if possible. Save the footage to show him when he gets out. He'll feel so guilty that he'll never leave you again'.*"

"That's nuts." Phil shook his head. "Eleanor, please put away your phone. Dr. Harper put together this nice dinner for us."

Let the angel voices ring!

"It's crazy," she said, biting into a forkful of steak. "Everyone told them to keep at it. I seriously think they're just going to keep stabbing each other indefinitely."

"That's the idea," I muttered under my breath as I scooped some potatoes onto my plate.

Yeah, I wrote those comments. And a few more.

Like I said before, revenge is petty. But sometimes justice needs a little nudge in the right direction.

He rules the world with truth and grace!

"Noah, could you please pass the turnips?"

End of Patient File #116

A Note on Noah

I understand that you may still have concerns about Noah's motives.

Trust me, I did too.

I have a bit of a paranoid streak in me, and this whole experience had me doubting Noah — again. But I'll tell you more about my previous suspicions in the following patient files.

For now, all you need to know is that Noah is a good human being. You do not need to worry about him. He's clumsy, but he's loyal and he has a heart of gold.

He stayed with me through more than one hundred clients — from Patient #114 to #220.

And I don't like to talk about Patient #220.

Choir Boy

Choir Boy

I realized that I haven't even shared my gender with you yet. This single part patient file will resolve that mystery.

"There are burn marks all around his penis!"

Elliot's mother, Ruth, sobbed into her handkerchief as he stared intently at the ground.

"Elliot," I said gently. "Can you tell me more about these burns?"

He continued looking down.

"He won't talk," said Ruth. "I was hoping he'd open up to a woman, since he's been afraid of the past two male therapists."

I nodded. "That's perfectly normal after abuse," I said. "Elliot, you can trust us, okay? We're just here to listen."

He didn't respond.

"Please show her." Ruth turned to Elliot. "Just the ones near your inner thigh."

Elliot shut his eyes.

"Please."

He reached for his shorts and pulled them up, just enough

for me to see his groin covered in red and white burn marks.

"That's okay," I said quickly. "I believe you both. You can put your shorts back down."

Ruth sniffled again.

"Do you have any ideas who might be doing this?" I asked her.

"Father Michael," she said, almost instantly.

"Is he a minister at your Church?" I asked.

"He's the choir conductor," she said. "Elliot has a beautiful voice. More solos than any other choir boy in the Church's history."

She beamed.

"He's a bit old to be a choir boy, isn't he?" I asked, reviewing his patient file. "Fourteen, right?"

"Yes," she nodded. "He's a late bloomer. It's a gift from God, blessing us with more of his music before puberty takes his voice from us."

Elliott began tapping his foot on the ground.

"Elliot, do you know Father Michael?"

He nodded.

"And is he the one who's hurting you?"

He shook his head.

"Then who *is* hurting you?"

He continued looking at the ground for a while, and then mumbled: "God."

"I'm sorry?"

"It's God." He looked up. "God is doing this to me."

Ruth began crying again. "You *have* to stop saying that, Elliot! It's blasphemous."

"Wait, hold on a minute," I said. "Elliot, can you tell me more about why you believe God is doing this to you?"

"I don't know."

"It's Father Michael!" Ruth shrieked. "The burns *always* appear after choir practice. Elliot's just confused, and blaming God for it, because Father Michael is a religious figure."

Surprisingly, I agreed with her initial assessment.

"Have you gone to the police with your concerns?"

She shook her head. "My husband won't allow it."

"Why?"

"Father Michael is an upstanding member of the community," she said. "If we're wrong, we'll be ostracized from the Church."

I thought for a moment, and then decided to turn my attention back to Elliot. I've gotten in trouble for jumping to conclusions in the past.

"Elliot, do you have any close friends?"

"Yeah," he said. "Zach. He's in the choir too."

"Have you told Zach about your burns?"

"No," he said. "But he helps me feel better after."

"That's good," I said. "It's great to have friends help us through difficult times."

But silently I wondered if Zach was being molested by Father Michael too.

"How does he help you feel better?"

"We go to the top of the bell tower after choir practice on Sunday nights," he said. "And we map out the stars."

"That sounds nice!" I said encouragingly.

"I know *all* of the constellations," he said proudly. "Even the ones that changed a thousand years ago. Zach only knows the big dipper and a few others."

"That's really cool," I said. "Elliot, would you mind if I spoke to your mother alone for a moment?"

He nodded.

I motioned for Ruth to step outside the office with me.

"Ruth," I began in a hushed voice. "I know your husband is opposed to contacting the authorities, but I have to insist—"

"Oh, we can't." She shook her head.

"Listen," I said more firmly. "I have reason to believe that your child is in danger, and we have a pretty good idea of who's doing it to him."

She looked at me with red eyes. "But what if we're wrong?"

"What if we're *not?*" I challenged. "What if Father Michael is out there hurting other kids too? Like Zach."

She bit down on her lip. "What do you want to do?"

"I want to call the police, and let them open an investigation," I said. "That's it. If he's innocent, fine. But if he's not, at least, he'll be away from the kids while they investigate."

Finally, she nodded.

It was Monday morning, and the police were holding Father Michael while they investigated Elliot's case. It gave me enough peace of mind to focus on my other patients, but I still couldn't stop thinking about Elliot.

I've seen this kind of sexual abuse before, but it's such a sadistic thing to do to a child. This type of thing can seriously mess up a young person for a long time.

I was just getting ready for another session when Ruth stormed into my office with Elliot.

"Ruth!" I said. "Our appointment isn't until next week."

It's really important to maintain boundaries with patients, otherwise they start calling your cell phone at all hours of the night.

"You were wrong!" she said. "He has another burn."

"Another one?" I said. "But Father Michael—"

"Thanks to you, he's been with the police since last week," Ruth hissed. "But a new burn appeared just last night after he came home from practice. Go on, Elliot, show her."

Elliot was about to pull up his shorts again, but I stopped him. "I believe you," I said. "I'm sorry I got it wrong. I just wanted to make sure he was safe."

"Well clearly he's *not* safe!" she hissed. "Isn't this your *job*? He won't talk to the police and he won't talk to me, so what are we paying you for?"

"You're right." I nodded. "I'm going to do better. I have a client arriving in a few minutes, but I'd like to spend more time with Elliot as soon as possible. I'm fully booked this week, but can he come in this weekend?"

"Yes," she said shortly. "Before choir practice on Sunday

night."

Elliot was staring at the ground again and shuffling his feet.

We were running out of time to save a boy's future – his body, his emotional health, his humanity.

"Thank you for meeting with me, Father Michael."

I know, I know... I shouldn't have come to their Church. But before I saw Elliot this weekend, I had to rule out Father Michael once and for all. He was still the most logical answer, and I couldn't shake the feeling that there might be other Church members involved.

"Of course," he said.

"I'm sorry for falsely accusing you," I said. "I was wrong."

"It's quite alright," he said, gesturing to the grand nave around us. "Ephesians 4:32... Be kind to one another, tenderhearted, forgiving one another, as God in Christ forgave you."

I gave him a short smile. "That's a nice verse."

"I understand why you did it," he said gently. "But I hope you can see now that a man of God would never initiate inappropriate contact with another male."

I found it a little unsettling that he seemed more concerned about the male thing than the 14 year old thing.

"Father Michael, are there any other members of the Church who you think could be doing this to Elliot?"

He gave me a dark look. "Yes."

I felt my adrenaline surge.

"Who?" I asked. "Please tell me so I can help him."

He took a long pause and then said, "Elliot's mother."

I accidentally let out a laugh. "Ruth?"

He nodded.

"That's impossible." I shook my head. "She's the one who brought him in to see me. Why would a mother ever do that to her own child?"

"A few months ago, I told her that Elliot would need to leave

59

the choir soon."

"Why?" I asked.

"Because his voice is changing," he said. "We have a beautiful adult choir that he would thrive in, but Ruth hated that idea."

"She insisted that he stay with the choir boys?"

"It was more of a threat than insistence," he said. "She started screaming at me and told me I was wrong about his voice changing, and that he would be a little boy forever."

"Wait, you don't think—"

"Yes..." he said gravely. "I got the sense she'd do *anything* to keep Elliot's voice from changing."

As I waited for Elliot and Ruth to arrive for our Sunday afternoon session, I felt like I wanted to crawl out of my own skin. I couldn't stop moving. Fidgeting. Thinking.

Finally, the doors opened.

"Thank you both for coming in," I said quickly, standing up to greet them. "Ruth, if it's okay with you, I'd like to speak with Elliot alone for this session."

"Absolutely not." She shook her head. "He needs me."

I cleared my throat. "The therapeutic process is actually more effective if—"

"I said no."

I felt my blood boiling. "Is that because you're the one hurting him?"

Oops.

"Excuse me?"

"The choir," I said. "You want to keep his voice this way forever."

"What— What are you implying?" Her voice got more shrill. "You think I would burn my boy's body for some *music?*"

"That's exactly what I think," I said. "Another horrible stage mom who forces her child to perform, just to make up for her own lifelong failures."

Her face was rapidly turning the color of a tomato, which I had to admit brought me some satisfaction.

"The police already ruled me out!" she screamed. "Father Michael fed them the same story, so they looked into it. We have home security videos that prove the latest burns appeared after practice last Sunday. *While I was home, and Father Michael was with the police.*"

I accidentally bit at my nails. *Damn it.* Therapists weren't supposed to have nervous habits.

The adrenaline was wearing off, and now I was starting to doubt myself.

"I'd like to take a look at your security videos."

"How dare you!" She grabbed Elliot and turned for the door. "We came to you for help, and it turns out you're just a judgmental bitch who can't do her job."

"If you'll just—"

"I'm getting a restraining order," she said. "And if you ever contact us again, I'll call the police."

She slammed the door behind them, and I sat in my office feeling incredibly embarrassed. Sometimes I get worked up — almost excited — by the idea of a big fight. But afterwards, I always feel ashamed. Especially when I'm wrong.

It was Sunday, so I didn't have any more appointments. And a restraining order didn't mean I had to stop *thinking* about Elliot. So I just sat in my office for hours, mulling over the information and trying to figure out what I had missed.

There could still be other members of the Church or choir hurting him. His dad could even be involved, but presumably the police had covered that possibility. I needed more time alone with Elliot. I had to learn about the other people in his life.

It took me a long time to realize that the sun had set, and that my room was now nearly pitch black.

I was about to check the time on my phone, but then the Church bells decided to help me out. As they rang out in the distance, I listened and counted from my office.

One. Two. Three. Four. Five. Six. Seven. Eight.

By eight o'clock, Elliot would be finishing his choir practice and heading up to the bell towers with—

And then suddenly, it felt like all of the blood had left my body.

I had completely forgotten someone who should have been a prime suspect the entire time.

Zach.

How had I missed this?

As I sprinted up the stairs to the bell tower, it all started making sense. Ruth said the burns always appeared after choir practice, but Elliot and Zach also came up here every night after choir practice.

Maybe "God" was the stars. Maybe Elliot was staring up at them every Sunday night while Zach burned him, and then he used "God" to mask the unbearable pain of his friend's betrayal.

"GET AWAY FROM HIM!"

At the top of the tower, I sprinted over to Zach and pulled him away from Elliot.

"Who *are* you?" said Zach.

"Why are you doing this to him?" I stood in between the two of them, facing Zach. "Why would you *ever* do this to your friend?"

Zach swallowed, fear in his eyes.

I lunged forward and shook him. "Tell me!"

"It's not him!" Elliot suddenly yelled out, eyes burning red.

"It has to be," I said. "Elliot, you don't have to be afraid of him anymore."

"I'm not afraid of him," he stammered. "I'm— I'm in love with him."

Zach looked at him, confused.

That made two of us.

In love…? With— him?

Oh. I sighed. *Of course.*

0 for 3. That had to be a new record for me. But this time, everything clicked – for real. If I had actually done my job and

spent more time listening to Elliot, we probably could have gotten here a lot faster.

"Zach, could you give us a moment alone?"

Zach nodded and walked over to the stairs.

"Elliot…" I put my hand on his shoulder. "What do you mean you're in love with Zach?"

"I can't help it!" he sobbed. "I've been trying to stop for so long."

"Elliot, are you trying to stop yourself from loving Zach?" I asked. "Are you the one burning your body?"

"Yes," he said, ashamed. "I thought it would make my feelings go away. I said it was God because I didn't want to get anyone into trouble. But you kept accusing everyone. And now – now Zach knows I'm bad."

I closed my eyes, pained by his pain. This wasn't a case of molestation. It was a story of first love, internalized homophobia, and self-flagellation.

"Bad?" I repeated gently. "Elliot, it's wonderful to love your friend."

"No it's not!" He raised his voice. "Leviticus 18:22, Timothy 1:8-10, Corinthians 6:9-10. They all say the same thing. It gets you thrown into Hell with murderers and liars and cheaters."

I shook my head angrily. He probably heard Father Michael recite verses like that every day. Who needs an abuser when you have a big book telling kids that an omniscient deity thinks they're defective.

"A real God would never punish you for having love in your heart."

He looked up at me desperately. "Because Jesus forgives me?"

"There is nothing *to* forgive, Elliot". I said, frustrated. "This isn't anything like murder and adultery. You haven't done anything wrong. You are wonderful as you are. Whole and good."

He hung head down. "Then why do I feel so bad?"

"Because of shame," I said. "Shame feels bad. You've absorbed messages about yourself that are not true, and your mind is tricking you into thinking that those messages are coming from God."

"But what if they *are* coming from God?" asked Elliot. "Isn't it better to be safe, so I don't go to Hell forever?"

"Can you imagine God creating this vast universe, full of oceans and mountains and stars and galaxies – and then being so petty that He punishes you for loving who you love?"

This was completely inappropriate, and unprofessional, and not at all my place. And yet, I continued:

"What if shame and fear are the only things blocking you from realizing who you truly are?" I said. "What if God is less of a punitive human figure, and more of an abstract energy that runs through all of us?"

"All of us?" he repeated curiously.

"Yes," I said, gesturing around me. "This tower is God. This Earth is God. The stars are God. Zach is God. I am God. *You* are God."

He stared at me with wide eyes, and then whispered: "*I am God.*"

Something about the way he said that made my skin crawl.

And then, in the glow of the moonlight, I saw his face light up. It was a combination of relief, euphoria, and… power.

I've seen the same look on a few other patients – when they finally shed all the darkness that blocks them from their greatest potential. But I've never seen it happen so fast, and I've definitely never seen it happen to a 14-year-old boy.

"Dr. Cole, when I grow up, I'm going to be just like you." He smiled, a tear running down his cheek. "I'm going to save everyone."

"That's very humbling," I said with a nervous laugh. "But we can't save everyone."

A shadow cast over his face. "Well *I'm* going to save *everyone.*"

I gave him an encouraging nod. It was touching, if not a bit unsettling.

He walked slowly to the edge of the tower and surveyed the stars. Then he leaned his head back and raised his hands into the night sky. In that moment, it was almost as if he commanded the Heavens themselves.

And then, with a fire burning in his eyes, he turned to me and spoke again:

"They'll call me Dr. Harper."

As the bells rang out above us, a shiver coursed through my body, even though it was the middle of summer.

I know it sounds strange, but I got the uncanny feeling that I had accidentally created a hero.

Or a monster.

End of Stolen Patient File - Elliot Harper, 14 Years Old

A Note on Elliot

For any readers confused by that ending, I am Elliot.

Dr. Cole was my childhood therapist. When I got older, I worried that a history of self-harm could hinder me from entering a career in medicine, so I stole the file from her.

Dr. Cole saved my life, and I regret stealing from her, but I hope she would understand why I did it. I also admit I "borrowed" her idea to write out each patient file, as well as her hot-headed temperament.

Don't worry, the rest of the patient files are mine. No more tricks.

For anyone wondering if my voice remained beautiful after puberty the answer is a resounding 'No'. It sounds like a cross between a seagull and a birthday kazoo. I still enjoy singing in the shower.

But most likely, you want to know how Zach reacted. Well, he was straight, so I got to experience my first heartbreak. But that's better than feeling nothing at all. Zach remains one of my closest friends to this day, and we go out for tea each month.

I have just three more patient files to share with you now. I've chosen these ones, because they all lead up to Patient #220, which is when everything went to hell.

PTSD Nightmares

PTSD Nightmares

PART ONE

"Known as '*The Zombie*', this terrifying new serial killer bites victims to death before feeding on their organs – mimicking tropes from zombie horror films. Primarily targeting young men, this elusive murderer has an entire state living in fear. With six victims and no leads, authorities encourage local residents to remain vigilant–"

I switched off the news and pushed my cereal across the table. Another breakfast ruined by CNN.

I locked up the house and drove to work, pleased to see Noah's car already in the parking lot. It took a long time, but he had grown into quite a good assistant – and he'd stuck around far longer than any of the others.

"Good morning, Noah."

"Hey, doc!" he said, hurrying over to take my coat. "Coffee?"

"No, thank you." I walked into my office and he trailed behind with his iPad.

"This morning, you have '*Mormon grandpa with nightmares*'," he said, scrolling across the screen. "Howard Prince, and his wife – Jane. Oh, and their grandson, Eric."

"What are the nightmares about?"

He scanned the screen again and shook his head. "It doesn't say."

"Thanks, Noah."

I began preparing my office for the morning. Three pillows on the couch today, one for each patient – assuming they wanted to sit together.

A few minutes later, Noah showed the family inside. On his way out, he placed a coffee on my desk and gave me a thumbs up.

I cleared my throat.

He turned around. "What's up, doc?"

He had a big smile on his face – so happy with himself for remembering the coffee I didn't ask for.

"Nothing," I said, smiling back. "Thanks for the coffee."

As he walked out of the office, I let out a sigh and took a sip from the mug.

When had I gotten so soft?

"The nightmares started two months ago," said Howard. "I'm always alone in a dark field, wandering around aimlessly. And I'm eating something, but I can't remember what."

He fiddled with his thumbs and moved his mouth around strangely, as if he was biting his tongue.

His wife, Jane, placed her hands on his – and the fiddling abruptly stopped.

Then Howard's grandson, Eric, spoke up. "Tell Dr. Harper what happens next."

Jane shook her head. "I don't think–"

"Come on, grandma," said Eric. "This is why we came to therapy."

"I don't judge," I said encouragingly. "Trust me, I've seen a lot of things. Nightmares are more common than you'd think."

Jane closed her eyes and let out a disapproving sigh.

"Screaming," said Howard quietly. "When I finally wake up, there's a lot of screaming."

"Howard, it's totally natural to have strong reactions to nightmares."

Howard shook his head grimly. "They're not my screams."

I leaned forward. "Whose are they?"

"I don't know," he said. "By the time it's all over, I've forgotten."

I frowned. This sounded a lot like parasomnia. But he said it only started a few months ago, and sleepwalking isn't usually something that kicks in at age 78.

"Have you noticed any behavioral changes that accompany these nightmares?" I asked.

"It's been really difficult," Eric answered for his grandfather. "He's become irritable and hypervigilant – and he seems detached from us."

That was interesting. Three textbook symptoms of PTSD, in addition to the nightmares.

"Howard, before the dreams started, can you recall any significant events? Possibly a trigger of some sort?"

He thought hard. "We were on a family vacation with Eric and the great grandkids up north. I was on an early morning walk with Jane, and that was the first time I blacked out. I've never blacked out before."

"Jane, do you remember this walk?"

"No," she said flatly, standing up. "This was a mistake. We shouldn't have come in today."

"Stop it, grandma!" Eric stood up too. "He needs help."

"He'll be fine," said Jane. "We're handling it in our own way."

"Right, the Mormon way," said Eric angrily. "Load him up with Prozac until he seems normal and happy."

"How dare you," hissed Jane. She reached for Howard's wrist. "Come on, Howard. We're leaving."

"Howard," I said calmly, trying to diffuse the tension. "You're presenting several signs of post-traumatic stress disorder, which is actually quite treatable. Of course I would need more time to make a formal diagnosis, but different techniques like EMDR or mindfulness could help you feel a tremendous amount of relief."

He turned to me curiously. "I thought PTSD was something that happens to soldiers who fought in wars."

"No, it can be any traumatic situation," I said, trying to keep his attention. "As a result, your body tends to contract or tighten up – replacing your regular emotions with numbness and agitation, and terrifying you in the middle of the night with scary dreams. It's a very painful way to exist."

"Why does the body do that?"

"Because it's trying to protect you," I said. "Think about a kid who touches a hot stove. His body and mind quickly learn to never do that again, right?"

"Right," said Howard. "But what does that have to do with PTSD?"

"The problem with PTSD is that the body and mind work on overdrive to prevent the same fear or pain from happening again. It's like repeatedly touching a hot stove to remind yourself that it hurts. It's stuck in a feedback loop."

"But what is it trying to protect me from?"

"That's exactly what we need to find out," I said. "But I need more time with you, and I'd prefer if we could meet one-on-one."

"That's *enough!*" said Jane. She pulled his arm and marched him out the door.

I wanted to stop them, but you can't force patients to accept your help. I learned that the hard way.

"Sorry," said Eric, hurrying after them. "I'll convince them to come back, I promise."

I sat there, feeling increasingly frustrated by the outcome of the session. I *hate* unsolved patient mysteries, and I got the sense Jane would never allow Howard back in my office.

A few seconds later, Noah appeared in the doorway.

"What happened?" he asked. "They were only in there for a few minutes."

"The grandmother – Jane," I said, fuming. "She wouldn't let him finish. It's like she just stole the whole conversation away from us."

Noah looked like he was thinking hard for a few moments, and then his face lit up. "It's convoluted".

I looked up at him impatiently. "What?"

"Stolen conversation," he said proudly. "Convo-looted."
I stared at him and blinked.
"Please get out of my office."

I'd finally reached the end of the day, but I was too distracted with Howard to offer much help to my other patients. When someone leaves before I can figure out their problem, it gnaws away at me like a parasite in my brain.

I began packing up my things and turned out the lights. When I got to the lobby, I was surprised to see that Noah was already gone. He never leaves before me.

Was he seriously offended that I dismissed him from my office? I mean, I've punched the guy in the face before, and he still stuck around.

Oh well. We'd figure it out in the morning.

I locked up the doors and started the long drive home. My house is in the middle of nowhere, deep in the woods with a winding driveway.

I love my privacy.

The only thing I don't like about the house is the separate garage. The builders apparently thought it would be neat to have the garage and guest house disconnected from the main house, which is all well and good — until you have to walk between the two at night.

I've dealt with some scary people in my life, but nothing frightens me quite like the path from the garage to my house. My mind starts playing tricks on me, convincing me that a stalker or a discouraged patient could be waiting in the woods for me.

As I stepped out of my car, I picked up my bag with one hand and shielded the view of the lawn and woods with my other hand. Don't judge. I've got it down to a science.

I hurried across the path, but then I saw something between my shielding fingers – an unexpected movement in the woods.

My body went cold.

"*It's all in your mind…*" I whispered to myself.

I picked up my pace, and then I heard an unmistakable choking sound.

"What the *hell*." I dropped my hand and spun around.

I fumbled with my phone and turned on the flashlight, shining it at the lawn.

The image I saw next is one that I'll never forget.

Standing there – on the edge of my lawn and the woods – was a hooded figure kneeling over something.

Or someone.

When the hooded figure saw the light of my phone, it raised its head to face me.

I couldn't see its eyes, but I could see its mouth.

It was chewing slowly, and dark chunks were spilling from its teeth to the ground.

PART TWO

"Why is it *always* your house, Elliot?"

Officer Donahue made his way into my kitchen after searching the woods.

"It's not like I *want* these visitors," I snapped.

"Well, we've searched the entire premises, and there's no sign of anyone," he said. "And certainly nothing on your lawn to indicate The Zombie killer was here eating someone—"

"Then what the hell was it eating?" I pressed, irritated that he wasn't taking me seriously. "There had to be something – some sort of food at least."

"Listen, we can check again in the morning," he said with a slight smirk. "But I promise you there wasn't any human flesh on your lawn. Maybe all those crazies are finally getting to your head?"

"*Oh, fuck you,*" I muttered under my breath.

"Excuse me?"

"I was just saying 'thank you'." I smiled back. "Now, it's late. I better be getting to sleep."

"Alright, doctor…" he said with an eye roll. "Have a good night."

I let him out the front door and double checked my locks from my phone (the whole system is digital).

Then I called Noah for the fifth time that night.

"*Answer your goddamn phone, Noah.*"

Voicemail again. Where the hell was he?

I gave up and then called Howard and Jane's home. This was another one of my not-so-ethical moments, but give me a break, the adrenaline was still surging.

"Hello?" It was Jane.

"Jane," I said. "This is Dr. Harper. I think I just received a visit from your husband."

"What are you talking about?"

"Someone was out on my lawn, eating something," I said. "It reminded me a lot of Howard's nightmares. And that Zombie guy all over the news."

"What— What are you implying?"

"I'm implying that I strongly recommend you both come in for an appointment tomorrow morning," I said. "Or I'll have no choice but to share my suspicions with the authorities. Everyone in town will hear the police sirens at your house."

"Are you— Are you blackmailing us into coming to therapy?"

"Not blackmail," I said. "Just a strong recommendation."

I hung up the phone and made my way up to bed. My mind was still going a million miles an hour. By 3am, my brain finally surrendered to my body's exhaustion.

But as I drifted to sleep, I was plagued by dreams of a hooded figure… kneeling over Noah… and tearing out his stomach.

I got to work early, hoping that Noah would be in early again. But his car wasn't in the parking lot.

I opened up the office and saw a note on his desk. I picked it up, but before I could start reading it, I felt someone behind me. I spun around, fist raised.

"Woah it's just me, doc!"

"Oh my god, Noah." I let out a big breath of relief and shocked myself by pulling him into a tight hug.

As soon as I realized what I had done, I backed away.

"Sorry about that," I said stiffly, brushing my sleeves. "I– I thought something had happened to you."

He broke into a huge grin. "Aww! You like me."

"No I don't," I said. "But I'm glad you weren't eaten."

"Eaten?" He raised his eyebrows. "I was just camping with my friends. That's why I came in early yesterday – so I could leave early. I left you a note!"

"Of course you did," I muttered. "Could you please get me some water?

"Sure!" He still had that big stupid grin on his face.

"And stop smiling like that," I snapped.

"Sorry, I can't help it," he called out from the bubbler. "You like me!"

"I don't like you!"

Jesus Christ. I sounded like a fucking middle schooler.

Jane was glaring daggers at me from the couch, but Howard and Eric seemed happy to be back in the office.

"Howard, did you have any nightmares last night?"

"Yes," he said anxiously. "During my evening nap."

"And what time was that?"

"I think around 8?"

Right when I got home. Shocker.

"Jane and Eric, do you monitor Howard when he sleeps?" I asked. "To ensure he stays safe?"

"We try," said Eric. "But sometimes we're both out of the house. I drive Uber at night to help pay the rent and insurance. And grandma needs to sleep too."

"Given the circumstances, you don't think a home security camera setup might be a good investment?"

"Absolutely not," Jane spoke up. "We don't need the FBI watching us in our homes."

I find it very obnoxious when people present problems with obvious solutions, dismiss the solution, and continue complaining about the problem.

"Howard, would you be willing to try EMDR today?" I asked. "There are varying opinions on it, but I've seen great results on past patients with PTSD."

"Okay." He nodded. "What is it?"

"Eye movement desensitization and reprocessing," I said. "Essentially we'll recall distressing memories, and then help you process them in a healthier way."

Some people think it's no more effective than a placebo, but that doesn't matter to me if it's producing results. It all just depends on the patient.

"What does the eye part have to do with it?"

"During REM sleep, your eyes move side-to-side rapidly. Using bilateral stimulation, we can replicate that state and get you in touch with subconscious feelings that may be unprocessed or repressed."

"This sounds dangerous!" said Jane.

"Howard is in a safe environment, and I'm here to help him walk through any traumatic emotions or memories that resurface."

"Come on, grandma," Eric pushed. "Let's give it a try."

She shook her head. "Fine. But we're staying with him."

"I'd actually prefer we do this alone—"

"That's not happening," she said firmly. "We all stay, or we all go."

I did my best to conceal my frustration. She was more stubborn than me, but I could still work with this.

As we began the session, I dimmed the lights and started the eye scanner. There are a lot of different tools for EMDR, but I like the eye scanner. It's basically just a horizontal set of small lights that stream back and forth.

Howard took to the scanner pretty quickly, which was a good sign.

After some initial warm up questions, I asked softly: "Howard, can you return to your family vacation up north?"

"Yes," he said, eyes moving back and forth with the lights.

"Can you return to your early morning walk with Jane?"

He paused for a moment. "Yes."

"What's the first thing you can remember before the blackout?"

He paused again. "We're walking along the road and we see a farm to our left."

"Very good," I said. "Can you tell me about that farm, Howard?"

"There are animals," he said. "Goats. Horses. And cows."

"Are there any people?"

"No." He shook his head.

"Are you certain?"

His eyes were moving quickly. Then they widened.

"There's a little girl," he said, suddenly looking panicked. "Oh god—"

"Howard, it's okay," I said calmly.

"No it's not!" he shouted. "Oh god, what am I doing?"

"That's enough!" Jane stood up and flipped on the lights.

"What the hell are you doing?" I yelled. "He's in a very vulnerable state."

"I'm filing a complaint," she said, forcing Howard off the couch. "Your license should be taken away."

"Eric, please talk sense into her," I said desperately. "It's very dangerous for him to leave in this state. At least give me a moment to ground him."

Eric looked conflicted, but then shook his head. "Sorry."

They left me standing there alone in my office, heart pounding.

I still had no idea what was going on with Howard.

And now he was more unstable than ever.

"Graphic new security footage has surfaced of The Zombie's latest murder. While we can't see the killer's face, it does shed light on a strange new behavior. In the video, we can clearly see The Zombie punching itself in the face after the attack—"

My car radio faded out to static. Damn it. That meant I was almost home.

It was still a bit light out, which made my house much less creepy. I was relieved to see no hooded figures on the walk from my garage to the house.

After locking up, I cooked myself a small dinner and spent the rest of the night reviewing my other patient files. I had fallen behind on everyone else, which I tend to do when I become obsessed with a patient.

Before going to bed, I brushed my teeth and looked out the bathroom window over my yard. The silhouettes of trees looked ominous, but everything seemed normal.

Until I saw a shadow on the edge of the lawn and woods.

I didn't have a tree there.

Heart racing, I took out my phone and called 911. Then I grabbed my gun and bolted downstairs. I was careful to be quiet when I opened the back door, hoping to sneak up on them unnoticed.

As I got closer, I recognized the same hooded figure from last night – kneeling on all fours, and feeding on something.

"Stop!" I shouted, pointing the gun and flashlight at it. "Don't move."

The figure looked up abruptly and revealed a familiar face.

"Howard?" I whispered.

It made no sense. How the hell could a 78-year-old grandpa be The Zombie? How could he possibly be overtaking strong young men and biting them to death?

"Don't move," I said again, carefully inching forward.

I shined my flashlight in his mouth, which was spilling over with more chunks of something.

But it wasn't human flesh.

It was grass and dirt.

And he was chewing in a strange slow sideways motion – almost like a cow.

Then he stared at me, tilted his head, and bellowed:

"*MOOOOOOO......*"

PART THREE

So... a patient who thinks he's a... cow... has been eating your... grass."

Officer Donahue slowly looked up from his police report. His expression was a mixture of annoyance and boredom.

"That's right," I said.

"Elliot, come on..." He sighed and closed the report. "You know, the guys at the precinct think I make this stuff up. And my wife laughs at me for dealing with this crap, while my buddies are out there searching for The Zombie."

"It's not crap!" I said. "The man has boanthropy."

He gave me a blank stare. "What's bone therapy?"

"*Bo-an-throp-ee*," I sounded out the syllables for him. "It's an extremely rare psychological disorder where the sufferer thinks they're a bovine."

Officer Donahue furrowed his brow. "Bovine..."

"Cattle animals," I said impatiently. "Cows, oxen, bulls."

Truth be told, my condescension was completely uncalled for. The only reason I even knew about boanthropy was because I once asked my childhood therapist what she thought the weirdest psychological disorder was. Boanthropy took the prize.

"Okay then..." he said. "So how did this... bovine escape from you?"

"By running away from me in the pitch black woods."

"Don't you have a gun?" he asked. "Why didn't you stop him?"

"I'm not going to execute a man for mooing at me," I snapped. "For God's sake, please just find him. He needs help, and he needs it fast. He's on the verge of a total mental collapse."

He sighed again, but then he rolled his eyes and leaned into his radio.

"This is Officer Donahue, requesting backup for the cow situation."

As Jane sobbed in front of me, I remembered the one thing I hate about being a therapist.

Not every psychological malady has a root cause or a solution. Sometimes it's just a combination of genetics, circumstance, and bad luck. There's nothing I – or anyone – can do to fix it.

"I'm so sorry," she said, wiping her eyes with a handkerchief. "I should have said something sooner. I just – I didn't want to believe it. After the first incident at the farm, I searched online and all the websites said it would start out as dreams, and eventually devolve into full-fledged insanity."

My heart sank. Jane wasn't some anti-therapy image-obsessed woman trying to prevent her husband from getting care. She was grieving. More specifically, she was in denial.

"When you started talking about PTSD, I got hopeful," she sniffled. "I thought maybe – maybe he had a chance. But he doesn't, does he? It's only going to get worse from here, right?"

Howard and Eric looked up from the couch, waiting for my answer.

Eric had a black eye from restraining Howard last night after he returned home. It pained me to see their family like this, and I didn't want to worsen things by delivering more bad news.

I took a deep breath. "Howard, have you been able to remember any of these episodes?"

"The EMDR helped," he said. "I remembered the farm. The little girl screaming as I crawled after her, making that horrible sound. And Jane crying hysterically – trying to stop me."

"It's really promising that you have some awareness of these incidents," I said encouragingly. "What about when you came to my house? Can you recall what guided you there?"

"I don't know." He shook his head.

"Take your time," I said. "Just like the EMDR, there's no pressure. No expectations. Just relax and see where your body takes you."

He nodded and closed his eyes. After a few moments, he spoke again. "When we left your office the other day, I saw your name and address on a package – on your assistant's desk."

I let out a small sigh. *Thanks a lot, Noah.*

"It said 'Happy Birthday Doc', so I guess he was planning to send you a gift or something," said Howard. "But when I saw your name, I just felt... drawn to you."

"Drawn to me?"

"Like – Like maybe you could help me," he said. "Even in that embarrassing state."

"I *am* going to help you," I said, turning to face the whole family. "But the first thing we need to do is drop the shame, okay? I want you all to think of Howard's illness like you would think about Alzheimer's. It's a progressive condition with no known cure, but there are plenty of steps you can take to provide him a decent quality of life."

"Like what?" asked Jane.

"I know you're opposed to the idea, but I highly suggest installing home monitoring equipment," I said. "Something that can alert you – or even lock your doors – when Howard is moving around unexpectedly."

Jane nodded seriously. "We'll do it."

"Great," I said. "And if you can afford in-home medical care, even just one day a week can help to greatly reduce the burden of caring for a loved one."

"I'll start driving extra shifts for Uber," said Eric, holding Jane's hand. "Anything we need to support him."

"Good," I said. "And there's one more thing."

They all nodded at once. It was inspiring to see them unite around Howard.

"I'd like to keep seeing Eric," I said. "Regular sessions, here in my office. Pro bono."

"Me?" Eric frowned.

"Similar to Alzheimer's, you have a genetic predisposition to mental illness."

His eyes widened with fear. "I'm going to get the cow issue?"

"That's highly unlikely," I said. "Odds are, nothing will happen at all. But there is an elevated chance that your genetics could activate in the form of some other condition – dissociation, blackouts, or even psychosis. So I want to ensure we take all possible steps to evaluate you and eliminate potential triggers."

He looked uncomfortable.

"It's better to be safe, Eric," said Jane. "Please give Dr. Harper a chance to check."

"Okay," he said. "I'm driving Uber this week, but I could take a day off next week."

"Great," I said. "I'll have Noah schedule you in."

As I helped them out of my office, I felt a pang of guilt in my core.

The truth was, Howard didn't have much time before he lost his mind entirely. Jane was correct that these nightmares would soon become Howard's everyday reality.

But seeing the family come together to help Howard gave me hope that he would at least enjoy his final days in the presence of love.

Boanthropy or not, most of us aren't so lucky.

———————————————————//———————————————————

Days later, I sat in my office and scrolled mindlessly through the news.

One familiar headline caught my eye: *Watch footage of Zombie Killer punching itself.*

I clicked it and watched with morbid curiosity as a covered figure attacked a young man behind an alley. It was hard to see much of anything since most of it was censored. After the young man stopped moving, The Zombie looked up and started shouting at the sky.

There was no audio, but you could clearly see The Zombie

raise its fist and start punching itself in the face.

Self-injury…. That was certainly interesting. That implied he felt some sort of remorse, which meant that he wasn't completely hopeless. Maybe he only attacked in some sort of dissociative state, and then felt horrified once he regained awareness?

I know, I know. This is a case for the FBI or the BAU. Not a therapist. But sometimes I can't help myself.

The news site automatically loaded the next video. It was the girlfriend of the latest victim.

"The last time I saw him, we were at the bar and he stepped outside for a smoke!" she said hysterically. "Then he got into a car and left. It had to be someone he knew, right? Why else would he just get into some random car?"

"Maybe a taxi," I mused out loud.

Then I felt a tingle surge up my spine. *Or an Uber.*

Oh my god. Eric was an Uber driver. And he had that black eye the other day, which he said came from restraining Howard. But he could have been lying. And mixed with a family predisposition for blackouts—

Before I could continue that train of thought, Noah opened the door and brought someone inside.

"Officer Donahue," I said urgently, standing up. "Your timing is perfect. I have a new theory about The Zombie."

"Well…" he said anxiously. "I'm actually here as a patient."

I raised my eyebrows. "Really?"

"Yeah, I mean you figured out that whole cow thing," he said, inviting himself over to the couch. "So I thought maybe you could help me with my wife. You see, she's a bit of a cow herself…"

Noah… I grumbled. How the hell did this make it through my 'interesting patients only' filter?

As Officer Donahue rambled on about his passive-aggressive wife and their unsatisfying sex life, I pretended to write in my notebook. My mind was somewhere else entirely. If Eric really was The Zombie, he was still out there driving Ubers. And it wasn't like Jane was in any position to stop him.

"So that's why I think I need help," Officer Donahue finished his story with a dramatic sigh.

"Spousal spats are completely normal," I said, trying to hurry along the discussion. "Perhaps you could bring her in next week for a couple's appointment? And while you're here, I actually have a potential lead on The Zombie—"

"No, I seriously need help!" he raised his voice, face going red. "You have to help me!"

I was surprised to see Officer Donahue's eyes brimming with tears.

And then, without warning, he bolted up from the couch and began screaming:

"I. DO. NOT. NEED. HELP."

Then he lifted his fist into the air and punched himself in the face.

"*No fucking way,*" I whispered, eyes going wide.

I scrambled to find a pen on my desk, and then I scrawled the start of a new patient file in my notebook:

"*Patient File #220: Officer Donahue*"

End of Patient File #219

A Note on Patient #220

Before we get to Patient #220, there is one more patient that I need to share with you:

Patient File #109.

This patient is from my earlier days, and they are undoubtedly the most dangerous person I've ever worked with. More than the school shooter, more than the cult, even more than #220.

You may be wondering if #220 will be the end of my patient files. It is my last patient file with Noah, but I do have other stories I can share with you someday.

It will all make sense soon.

Abusive Couple

Abusive Couple

"The most reliable sign, the most universal behavior of unscrupulous people is not directed, as one might imagine, at our fearfulness. It is, perversely, an appeal to our sympathy."

Martha Stout, The Sociopath Next Door

PART ONE

They had to be the youngest married couple I've ever worked with.

Her eyes were red with tears.

His eyes were exhausted and defeated.

"I think I should start..." Kierra sniffled through tears. "It's just so hard to ask for help, you know?"

"I understand," I said. "Why don't you begin by telling me what brings you to my office today?"

Kierra took a deep breath and nodded slowly. "He–" she stammered. "He hurts me."

I was surprised to hear Lucas groan from the corner. "Here we go again..."

"Don't do that!" Kierra shrieked. "You promised you would be honest here!"

"So did you," Lucas shot back. "But apparently we're just here to agree that I'm an abuser – like all of your other *abusive exes*, right?"

Kierra let out a loud sound – a mix between a sob and a

shout. "They *were* abusive!"

"Right, and I *saved* you from them," said Lucas bitterly.

"Until I became your latest abuser."

"DON'T DO THAT!" Kierra screamed. "You are invalidating and minimizing my experience!"

Good lord…

"Let's just take a step back here," I said, scooching my chair closer to distract them from each other. "Lucas, would it be okay if we let Kierra finish her story? I understand these are extremely serious allegations, but I assure you I will not rush to judgment until I hear your side too, okay?"

He nodded, although his expression was not one of agreement.

"Thank you," Kierra stammered. "It is so hard to speak my truth when he belittles me."

Lucas opened his mouth, but I gave him a sharp look and he backed down.

"Kierra, you just said that Lucas hurts you," I said. "Can you tell me more about that?"

She nodded and her eyes started welling with tears again. "It's a type of– a type of punishment."

"Punishment?" I asked. "What kind of punishment?"

She winced and whispered, "The Slicer."

"The Slicer?" I repeated. "What does that mean?"

She shook her head and buried her face in her hands. "I don't want to talk about it."

"That's okay," I said quickly. "Kierra, can you tell me more about what leads to this punishment?"

She looked back up. "Yes," she said. "He becomes angry when I call him out on his manipulation."

"What kind of manipulation?"

"It's subtle," she said. "It's called covert narcissistic abuse, and he fits all the red flags. Insensitive to my feelings, never apologizes or admits fault, needs constant attention from others–"

"Oh, for Christ's sake–"

"Just another moment, Lucas," I said, holding up my hand.

"I promise we'll get to you soon. Kierra, can you give me some examples of the manipulation?"

"Well, he's bisexual," she sniffled. "And he spends almost all of his free time with his gay friend."

"Do you see what I'm saying?" Lucas turned to me, exasperated. "This is her version of *abuse.*"

"Who spends that much time with a gay guy!" she shouted.

"He's my *friend!*"

"No, you do it to punish me!" she said. "It's a reminder that I'll never be enough to fully satisfy you. A warning that if I step out of line, you can always replace me in a heartbeat."

"Has there been infidelity?" I asked.

"No," said Lucas. "I would never—"

"Who knows!" Kierra interrupted him. "He's like your little pet. You parade him around on social media just to make me jealous. You never post pictures of us."

Lucas looked at me incredulously. "Do you get it now?" he said. "Do you see how crazy this is?"

Just as I was about to begin asking Lucas some questions, the door to my office opened.

"Oh, sorry."

A young, awkward looking man in a FedEx uniform stood in the doorway, holding a few brown Prime boxes

"Your front door was open. I heard voices in here. Wasn't sure if you wanted to sign, or…" He looked around the room, finally noticing Lucas and his tearful wife. "Oh, it seems like this might not be a great time?"

"*You don't say…*" I muttered, standing up to sign for the packages. "Just leave them in the lobby please."

He blushed and nodded, closing the door behind him.

God, I needed an assistant.

"Sorry about that," I said, sitting back down. "I just moved into this office, so things have been a little chaotic. Anyway, Lucas, I'd like for you to share your side of the story now."

"Okay," he said quietly. "Well first of all, I think she might be the one abusing me. She grabs me sometimes."

"I DO NOT!"

"Kierra," I said firmly. "Now we're going to give Lucas a chance to share."

She looked like she was going to explode.

Lucas rolled up his sleeves, revealing a series of bruises. "She grabs me when I try to leave after a fight," he said. "She accuses me of abandoning her."

"HE'S LYING!" Kierra shrieked. "He does that to himself!"

"I'm just really afraid," he continued. "I asked for help on a forum, and a lot of people suggested she might have Borderline Personality Disorder. I Googled it and she has almost every symptom – crazy mood swings between sobbing and rage... thinks everyone is abusing or traumatizing her... a new crisis story every hour... and I swear to God, any 'slicing' is 100% self-harm."

"More armchair diagnosis!" she cried.

"Are you serious?" He threw his hands into the air. "You just called me a narcissist!"

"Look, you've obviously both done some research on the internet," I said. "But perhaps it would be better if we met separately? That way you each have a chance to share your side, uninterrupted?"

"No!" They both protested at once.

I raised my eyebrows.

Then, at the same time, they spoke nearly the identical sentence:

"He'll manipulate you." / *"She'll manipulate you."*

My eyes scanned back and forth between the two of them curiously.

Hysterics versus irritation. Tears versus eyerolls. Slicer versus bruiser.

Were their online diagnoses correct? Was this really the age-old dance between The Borderline and The Narcissist?

Or was one of them lying?

For the rest of the session, I listened to them make more accusations – and more denials. To be completely honest, I still had no idea what was going on with them. If either of them was really in the Cluster-B spectrum (narcissist, sociopath, borderline, histrionic), it would take far more time to unravel the truth among all the manipulation and gas-lighting.

I actually have an optimistic view of Cluster-B recovery, but it's not going to happen with talk therapy, and it's certainly not going to happen in the midst of a dramatic relationship. That's like asking an alcoholic to begin recovery in the middle of a liquor store.

At the end of the session, I stood up to walk them out of my office. Lucas exited first.

Then, in the doorway, Kierra quickly leaned into my ear and whispered:

"He's going to kill me."

I'll admit, that sent chills down my spine. When it comes to domestic violence, you never want to take statements like that lightly. So when I closed the door to my office, the first thing I did was reach for the phone to involve the police.

But before I finished dialing, something caught my eye.

There was a piece of paper sticking out from the couch cushion – where Lucas had been sitting. I really didn't want them to come back later for a forgotten belonging, so I hurried over to examine it.

But when I unfolded the piece of paper, I didn't find a forgotten belonging

Instead, I saw a hand-scrawled note:

"She's going to kill me."

PART TWO

The following week, I set up my office for Lucas and Kierra's return.

But only one of them showed up.

"Lucas," I greeted him. "It's nice to see you. Will Kierra be joining us?"

He looked down and mumbled, "Not today."

"I'm sorry to hear that," I said, trying to mask my anxiety. The police hadn't found anything of concern last week, so I just needed to have faith that she was safe. "Did something come up?"

He took a seat in the couch and sighed. "We had a big fight last night."

"I see," I said. "About therapy?"

"Yeah." He nodded. "I wanted to come back, so we could work on our relationship. But she said you've already taken my side, so she didn't want to come back."

"I'm not looking to take sides," I said. "This isn't about winning or losing. A relationship should be a partnership, not a battle."

"That's what I keep telling her!" he said. "Sometimes it seems like she understands – like she wants to work on things with me – but then an hour or a day later, she does a 180 and thinks I'm trying to hurt her. I never even know what I did to make her switch."

I let out an uneasy breath. I still didn't know who to trust, but Lucas was the one who came in today, so he was the one I would try to help.

"You can spend a lifetime trying to manage her emotions – tweaking your own behavior to avoid her outbursts – but it won't make any difference if she still has a wound inside of her."

"What do you mean?"

"It's the difference between symptom management and root cause identification," I said. "Imagine a bucket with a hole in the bottom. What you're doing is repeatedly trying to fill the bucket, and then feeling inadequate when all the water leaks out."

"So how do I patch the hole?"

"You can't," I said firmly. "It's an internal problem that only she can solve, with the help of a professional. Right now, she's doing symptom management too. Her illness is convincing her that if she can arrange her surroundings just right – find a knight in shining armor, a perfect romantic partner – she will finally feel okay. But that is just using *external* distractions to fill her *internal* void. Her emptiness."

"She talks about emptiness all the time!" he said.

"I'm not surprised," I said. "Emptiness and boredom live under the surface of almost every Cluster-B disorder. I believe that's where the true wound lives, numbed out by all of these distractions. I would need far more time with Kierra to make any diagnosis, but if your suspicions are correct, you will have a long and rocky journey ahead."

He looked down. "You must think I'm an idiot for staying."

"I don't think that at all," I said. "But instead of focusing on Kierra today, I want to focus on you."

When it comes to abusive relationships, I try not to convince the victim that their partner is bad. Often times, that causes them to stop seeking help – especially early on, when they're dealing with cognitive dissonance about their abuser. Instead, I try to help the victim see their own value. Once we rebuild the self-respect and self-worth, everything else tends to fall into place.

I didn't have enough information to keep talking about Kierra, but exploring Lucas's self-esteem couldn't hurt – regardless of who was telling the truth.

"Lucas, do you feel hyper-aware of other people's emotions?" I asked. "Perhaps you can sense when someone's getting unhappy – or a conflict is brewing – so you step in to defuse it?"

"Yeah, exactly!" He lit up. "How did you know that?"

"The most common partner of someone with Borderline Personality Disorder isn't the Narcissist," I said. "It's Codependency. Caretaking. People pleasing. Rescuing. People who feel responsible for the emotions of others, burdened by constant guilt and worry when conflicts arise."

"Can I change that?"

"Of course," I said. "But before you can change it, you have to explore where it came from. Usually these habits start in childhood."

"Well, I had a really good childhood," he said, leaning back. "Both of my parents loved me. There definitely wasn't any abuse."

"It doesn't have to be abuse," I said. "Just someone who took up a lot of space. Emotional outbursts, constant fights, rigid rules, drinking issues, unpredictable moods... Anything like that?"

I know it's important not to ask leading questions, but codependents are likely to tell you they had perfect childhoods. With this approach, at least something might resonate with him that he wouldn't have otherwise considered.

"Holy crap, that's my dad!" he said. "He always had to be right about everything. Things would escalate from 0 to 100 for no reason. I think sometimes he actually enjoyed arguing."

"And how did that make you feel?"

"Well, it really upset my mom," he said. "She would get sad and cry. Sometimes they'd even shout at each other."

"But how did that make *you* feel, Lucas?"

"Bad," he said quietly. "I just wanted them to stop. So I'd make jokes, and I'd usually comfort my mom afterwards to make her feel better. She was a lot more sensitive than him."

"You learned to sacrifice your own needs to take care of others," I said. "To prevent conflicts and keep negativity at bay. And now that's how you approach relationships. But it's never enough, is it?"

"Never."

"That's because their issues have *nothing* to do with you," I said. "You can't change or save them."

"So what can I do?"

I reached into my desk and took out one of my favorite diagrams.

"This is the Karpman Drama Triangle," I said, handing it to him. "It has 3 corners: Victim, Perpetrator, and Rescuer."

"I'm the rescuer?" he asked.

"You're all of them," I said. "When we carry these wounds, we continue entering relationships and repeating the same story. Maybe we start as the rescuer, but our victimized partner inevitably comes to see *us* as the perpetrator. So we become the bad guy in their eyes. Then we're so exhausted and drained that we start to feel like the victim ourselves."

He shook his head in disbelief. "You're describing all of my relationships."

"Right, and it will keep happening until you see the triangle for what it is," I said. "A false version of love. Love is not heavy and sad. It is not pitiful and tragic. Love is light – infinite and open. It flows freely from within."

"But my heart feels so heavy," he said, "Like a big ball of dread and self-doubt. How can I ever change that?"

For the rest of the session, I provided him with books and printouts about codependency. I'm a big fan of the firehose approach when it comes to introspection. Eventually, something's bound to click.

When our time was up, I stood up to walk him out of the office.

"If you can, please bring Kierra with you next week," I said. "I'm confident that we can help her too."

He nodded. "I'll try."

I opened the front doors for him and began unpacking some of the boxes in my lobby. I still hadn't found an assistant, but at least I would be ready when the right resume appeared.

Before I could make much progress, someone knocked on the front door. It was the FedEx guy again, and he was carrying two more packages.

I let him in and signed for the delivery.

"Did you turn your patient gay?" he said with a laugh.

"What are you talking about?" I asked.

"Uh, sorry." He went red. "It's just, last week he was with a girl. Today he left with a guy. And they kissed. So I guess I was making a joke?"

I frowned. "He kissed another man?"

"Yeah, right after he got into the car," he said. "One of those old PT Cruisers. Man, those are goofy looking cars–"

I ushered him out the front door and ran to my car in the parking lot. I saw a PT Cruiser on the main road, heading south.

After running a stop sign and cutting off a few cars, I was a comfortable distance behind them. I followed the car off the highway and into the suburbs.

My mind was going a million miles a minute. If Lucas was lying about the infidelity, what else was he lying about?

I had latched so strongly onto this idea of Borderline and Codependent, I practically fed him everything I expected to hear.

But now I was re-thinking everything.

What if Kierra didn't have Borderline Personality Disorder at all? Partners of narcissists and sociopaths often develop Complex PTSD, which can look a *lot* like BPD. That's what happens when one person manufactures jealousy and insecurity in a partner. Sociopaths love to play innocent while their victims self-destruct and question their own sanity.

And even if Kierra had BPD, she certainly didn't deserve to be deceived and betrayed. She deserved a chance at happiness, just like anyone else.

The car finally slowed down and pulled into a driveway, so I stopped a safe distance before.

I saw Lucas lean in to hug the driver. Then he stepped out of the car, walked up the driveway, and headed into the garage as the car drove away.

Consumed by curiosity and distrust, I stepped out of my car and closed the door quietly. Then I snuck through the woods and approached the garage from the side.

I peered into the window and saw Lucas wandering toward

the back of the garage – with a kitchen knife.

And that's when I saw Kierra.

She was bound to a chair with rope, and her mouth was covered by duct tape.

She squirmed as he approached. My heart raced as I desperately tried to think of a plan.

Then Kierra looked up and saw me through the window.

Nothing came out of her mouth, but her eyes were screaming for help.

PART THREE

As Lucas approached Kierra – knife in hand – I realized the police wouldn't get here in time. I looked around the yard frantically. All I could find was an axe laying on top of a tree stump.

"*Fuck.*" I shook my head and ran over to grab it.

Without thinking twice, I sprinted back to the garage and burst through the door

I waved the axe around and shouted, trying to look and sound as intimidating as possible. Lucas was lanky, but he was in good shape. And he was probably around five years younger than me, so I needed an advantage on him.

They both looked completely shocked as I ran toward them.

"Drop the knife!" I shouted, brandishing the axe at Lucas. "Get the fuck away from her!"

He glanced one more time at Kierra, then at the door. He didn't drop the knife, but he ran around me and bolted out of the garage.

I dropped the axe and hurried over to Kierra, who was sobbing uncontrollably. As I got closer, I noticed a horrible smell. My heart sank as I realized she had soiled herself.

"You're okay," I consoled her as I untied the ropes. "You're safe now, okay? No one can hurt you."

She nodded through more tears.

"You're so brave," I continued talking calmly, trying to keep her attention on my eyes. "You're going to be okay."

Once she was free from the ropes, I draped my jacket over her shoulders and helped her from the chair.

"I need to call the police now," I said, taking out my phone. "I'm still right here with you, okay?"

"No!" she said, eyes going wide. "They'll arrest him!"

"Yes," I said. "Lucas will be charged."

"You can't!" she pleaded. "You can't get him into trouble."

I bit my lip. Victims of domestic abuse often cover for their partners, no matter how bad the abuse gets. It can take a long time to unravel that level of confusion.

"Kierra, because he put you in immediate physical danger, I have to call the cops," I said. "I promise everything is going to be okay."

"Please." She shook her head. "If he goes to jail, I think I'd – I'd kill myself."

In that moment, I considered hospitalizing Kierra for suicidal thoughts, but I was seriously concerned that her lingering attachment to Lucas would lead her right back into his arms once they were both free. I've helped a lot of patients break free from that trauma bond, so I came up with another idea.

"What if you come stay with me?" I asked. "I have a panic room above my garage. It's fortified with steel and blastproof Kevlar panels. You'd be untouchable."

She looked up and sniffled. "You'd let me stay there?"

"Yes," I said. "And if you'd like, I can provide you with daily therapy sessions until you're feeling better."

She paused for a moment and nodded. "Really?" she said. "Thank you – thank you so much."

"Great," I said. "Now, let's get you out of here – and find you a fresh set of clothes."

She buried her face, ashamed. "I'm sorry," she said. "That's the slicer."

"What do you mean?"

"He – He bakes these pies," she said. "And then he makes me slice off a piece and eat it every time I misbehave."

My jaw dropped in disgust. "And the pies are poisoned?"

"Yes," she said miserably. "They give me unbearable cramps and stomach problems. But I'm afraid someday it will be worse."

I bit my lip again. There was no way in hell that I'd ever let her return to Lucas. I'd keep my promise to her for now, but the moment she was ready to leave my place, I was going to call the police.

And if they didn't lock him away, I'd take matters into my own hands.

If I wasn't going to involve the cops yet, there was one more person I needed to protect. He wasn't hard to find, because – just as Kierra mentioned – Lucas had tagged him in dozens of public Facebook photos.

"Ryan," I stood up to greet Lucas's friend. "Thank you for coming in."

"Sure," he said, taking a seat. "You said it was urgent?"

"Yes," I said. "Your friend Lucas. He's extremely dangerous."

"Lukey?" He let out a small laugh. "I don't think so."

"You have to trust me," I said. "He was holding his wife in the garage – with the intent to harm her."

His eyes went wide. "You know about that?"

My heart started to race. Oh god, were they both in this together?

I slowly reached for the phone in my pocket. Enough was enough. It was time to stop playing detective and bring in the real police.

"It's not what it looked like," he said quickly. "He was just trying to protect her."

I lifted my fingers from the phone. "What?"

"She's crazy." He shook his head. "This whole therapy thing was his idea. He wanted to save their marriage, but she hated it. After the first session, she threatened to kill herself if he went back. She held a knife to her arm."

"You're lying."

"I'm not!" he said. "Listen, Lukey made some bad choices, but he's not a bad guy. He did it because he loved her."

"Yeah, I've heard that before," I scoffed. "Every abuser says they have to hurt their victim because of *love*."

"It's not like that!" Ryan protested. "He came back to you

because he wanted to keep getting help. He restrained her so she wouldn't hurt herself while he was gone. It was her idea—"

I crossed my arms.

"I swear to God!" he said. "She has some freakish addiction to being the damsel in distress."

"How do you even know any of this?"

Ryan looked down. "Because he asked me to watch her that morning," he said. "To make sure she was safe."

"Bullshit," I said. "He had a fucking knife."

"Probably to cut the rope!" said Ryan.

"What about the bowel movements?" I said. "The poisoned pies."

"I – I don't know," he said nervously. "She kept shitting herself and blaming his pies. This has been a thing for months now. She gets horribly sick every time he starts seeking help – from friends, family, and now you."

"You think she poisons herself *intentionally*?"

"I have no idea," he said. "But I tried a slice, and nothing happened to me."

I looked at him for a moment and shook my head.

"I'm sick of being lied to," I said, taking out my phone. "I know you're romantically involved with Lucas. This is all just some sick plot to get rid of Kierra, and I'm putting an end to it."

He frowned. "I'm not involved with Lukey."

"Yes you are," I said. "You kissed him in the parking lot."

His cheeks went pink. "You saw that?"

"Yes," I lied. It was true enough. "So now I know you're a liar too. Just like him."

"No, the kiss happened!" he said quickly. "But it was unreciprocated. I was just trying to show him what real love could feel like."

"Unreciprocated?"

"Yeah, I initiated it. But he pushed me away as soon as our lips touched." He looked down at the floor. "He has a heart of gold, but he's loyal to a fault. I don't think he'll ever escape the hold she has over him."

I looked at his eyes, trying to get a read on this whole

situation. I was seriously sick of the mind games and manipulation. This was why most therapists opted not to treat the Cluster-B disorders.

I stood up to indicate that our conversation was over. Now I was glad that I hadn't called the police, because there seemed to be a lot more to the story. I still had no idea who was telling the truth, but Kierra was safe above my garage, so I had plenty of time to figure this out.

After Ryan left, I sorted through some of the latest resumes for my assistant position. There were plenty of decent candidates – mostly grad students looking to get some experience – but none of them felt quite right.

There was a knock on the door and I looked up to see the FedEx guy back with another box.

That was strange. I wasn't expecting any deliveries today.

"Hey, doctor!" he said with a smile. "I tried to drop this off at a house in the suburbs, but the guy said his wife doesn't live there anymore. He said you might know where she is?"

I raised my eyebrows and took the package.

"I wonder if the wife left because you made him gay?" he said. "I mean, no offense, but that's not really a good outcome of couples therapy, right?"

I looked up from the package and glared at him. "Do you *ever* stop talking?"

He blushed and waved goodbye, which instantly made me feel bad for being so rude.

"Uh – Sorry," I said. "It's been a rough week. What's your name?"

"That's alright!" he said. "I'm Trevor."

"Thanks for everything, Trevor," I said. "You've made this whole move a lot easier for me."

He smiled again and said, "No problem!"

After he left, I looked down to the package addressed to Kierra. It really made me nervous that Lucas had referred the package to my office.

I would bring it to her, of course, but I had to examine it first. There was no way I'd let an unknown package into my safe room. I kept that place locked down like a bank.

I cut the package open and was surprised to pull out a package of gummy bears.

At first they seemed harmless, but then I read the label.

"*Oh, for fuck's sake...*" I could practically feel my blood pressure rising.

Kierra didn't have Borderline Personality Disorder or C-PTSD, and she definitely wasn't the victim of a sociopath.

"Kierra, you received a package today," I said, sliding the gummy bears her way in the panic room.

"Oh, thank you!" she said. "How was your day? I've been practicing all of the meditations you gave me, and they're helping so much."

Her eyes started brimming with tears again. "I just can't believe you've given me a second chance at life," she said. "I feel like I'm finally ready to start standing up for myself."

"That's great," I said flatly. "Why don't you have a gummy bear?"

She sniffled and looked at me, confused. "Right now? I'm not really hungry."

"Oh, I really have to insist," I said.

She shifted in her seat uncomfortably.

"What's the matter?" I said. "Not in the mood to vomit out your ass today?"

"What are you – What are you talking about?" The tears fell freely from her eyes.

"Nobody's poisoning you," I said. "Sugarless Haribo gummy bears? I had these on an airplane once – and it's an experience I'll never forget. There are about 300 Amazon reviews detailing similar experiences. So cut the fucking bullshit."

I was surprised to see her tears and hysterics stop abruptly.

"Congratulations," she said calmly. "You cracked the case of the diarrheal gummy bears."

I looked at her, trying not to appear anxious. It was

important to maintain the upper-ground with people like this.

"Has this all just been an act?" I asked. "You can just – turn off those emotions?"

"Well, they're always off," she said. "But yeah, I realized that Borderlines get more attention and sympathy, so I decided to give it a try."

A sociopath pretending to have Borderline Personality Disorder. That had to be a first.

"That's disgusting," I said. "There are people out there struggling with mental illness – trying so hard to get better – and you use it as a tool?"

She laughed. "Don't get all sanctimonious on me, dick burner."

I froze. "What did you say?"

"You burned your dick as a kid," she said matter-of-factly. "Is that why you're so obsessed with saving people? Because your first love rejected you, and now no one will ever love your burnt dick?"

I felt an intense dread forming in my stomach. I forgot about the files I'd left up here

"Where–"

"No need to freak out," she said, reaching forward to hand me the file. "But you know, we're actually pretty similar."

"No, we're not," I said, snatching the file away from her.

"Think about it," she said. "We're both puppet masters and control freaks. We both feel superior and safe when we're arranging everyone to do what we want."

"That's disgusting," I said again.

"No, it's incredible!" she said, eyes lighting up. "When I first met Lucas, he was so innocent and full of life. Cheerful and funny. Now he's angry, moody, and depressed – all for me."

"Well, I'm going to help him feel good again," I said. "So I guess we're not so similar."

"Please," she said. "You have no power over him. He's bonded to me, and he'll do whatever I say. He's like a little puppy. Even when he knows I'm fucking with him, he comes running back. He'll stay with me forever."

"He'll realize he deserves better," I said confidently. "Once we build up his boundaries and self-respect, he won't put up with your behavior anymore."

"That's when I give him the honeymoon phase again," she said with a smile. "Back when everything was perfect and we were 'soulmates'. That's the high he keeps chasing."

I felt my blood boiling. "I'm going to report you."

"To who?" She laughed. "The gummy bear police? There aren't any laws against emotional abuse. And if the police ever come knocking on our door, my body will be covered in enough bruises and scars to make sure he's the one leaving in handcuffs. Who would believe him over sad, wounded Kierra."

Her eyes began to tear up again, lip quivering. Then she stopped immediately and grinned.

"People like you are the reason that abuse victims are afraid to come forward," I said. "99% of the time they're telling the truth, but the world focuses on the 1% of liars like you."

"Hey, let's make a bet." She leaned forward, ignoring me. "I'll bet you $1,000 that by the end of the year, I can get Lucas to kill himself."

"That's murder."

"Not in the eyes of the law." She stood up to gather her belongings. "Now, I think I'll be checking out of the Harper Hilton. My husband needs me."

And then suddenly – without warning – I felt an overwhelming burning sensation tear through my heart.

Nothing good ever comes from that feeling.

Weeks later, Lucas returned for his twelfth daily session. That might seem like overkill, but it's really hard to break the addiction to a toxic person – so I wanted to be there for him, every step of the way.

"I just can't believe it!" he said, a big smile on his face. "I never thought I could feel like this. It's like my whole body weighs nothing. All the anxiety is just... gone."

"That's great, Lucas," I said. "I take it the guided meditations are helping?"

"All of it!" he said. "The meditations, the books, our sessions, all of it. It just feels like my heart is so big and free, you know?"

I broke into a rare smile too – I couldn't help it. Moments like this were exactly why I got into therapy. It was so inspiring to see Lucas transform his depression and anger into a joyful new chapter of his life.

"Oh man, I just want to dance around!" he said. "Do you like to dance?"

"Absolutely not." I shook my head. "But feel free to do a solo."

As he bounced around the room, I could practically see the energy bursting from the heart he was so proud of.

"You know," he said, slowing down. "When Kierra left me that breakup letter, I thought I would never be happy again. But now I feel a totally different kind of happiness."

"Do you miss her?" I asked.

"I don't know," he said, pacing around. "The letter was so thoughtful, and it made me realize she really is a good person deep down, even if we aren't together. The way she told me to move on and find joy without her... It was just so selfless."

I felt a bit guilty. I was the one who typed out that letter. But the ends justify the means, right?

Still, Kierra's *puppet master* comment nagged in the back of my mind.

"But then there are so many other things I don't miss," he said. "The drama, the fighting, the tricks... I don't feel like I'm walking on eggshells anymore. And you know something else weird? She never introduced me to her family. I want to be with someone who's excited to introduce me to their family!"

"That's great," I said, glad that he hadn't forgotten her darker qualities. "You deserve that."

"You really changed my life."

"Well, I also chased you with an axe," I said. "But I appreciate that."

He continued pacing around my office. "Do you think Kierra will ever come back?"

"I don't know," I said stiffly. "If she does, what would you do?"

"I guess I'd hear her out," he said. "She's probably working on herself too, right?"

I felt that dread in my stomach again. "Lucas, she was extremely abusive to you. People like that don't change overnight."

"I guess, but I would want to give her the benefit of the doubt!" he said. "And then she'd be able to see how well I'm doing too."

I pursed my lips. "In your particular situation, I'd exercise a lot more caution."

"What do you mean?" He frowned.

"Lucas, she wanted to cause you harm," I said, anxiety kicking in. "I actually think it might be a good idea to take measures to protect your identity."

He raised his eyebrows. "My identity?"

"That's right," I said. "People with Cluster-B disorders are notorious for returning and wreaking havoc in their victim's lives, even years after the relationship has ended."

"So you don't think Kierra could change?"

"I don't know," I said, growing increasingly agitated. "But for now, I'd really recommend changing your address, your career, and your name."

"My name?" He laughed.

"I'm serious," I said. "Please, will you just trust me?"

"Okay..." He nodded slowly. "I mean, you got me this far. I'm not going to start doubting you now. But there's no way I'll find a new job any time soon. I didn't finish college."

"You can come work for me," I said, surprised by the words coming out of my mouth. "I need an assistant."

"Really?" His face lit up. "Wow, sure. That would be awesome! You won't regret it. I'm going to be the best assistant you've ever had! Hey, we'll be like the Batman and Robin of psychology."

"Sure," I said. "Sounds like a plan."

If he was here, at least I could keep an eye on him for the majority of the week. And I could definitely upgrade the security around here.

"For my name, how about something unique..." he said, gazing off into the distance. "Like Dutygreen Weatherfancy."

"Dutygreen– What?" I sputtered. "No. The whole point is to pick something that won't draw attention to you. Here, just go with something from a list of common boy names."

I took out my phone and read off a few to him. "Liam... William... Noah... James..."

"Oh, I like Noah!" he said. "Noah Weatherfancy..."

"*Jesus Christ*," I muttered.

But before I could look up last names, Lucas – or Noah – pulled me into a tight hug.

"Thank you so much, Doc," he said. "You didn't just save my life. You made it a life worth living."

I looked into his eyes – eyes that were so eager, and so kind. Suddenly, I felt an extremely warm, soft vulnerability in my heart – an unexpected sensation I hadn't known since childhood.

So in that moment, I decided I would need to shut him out of my heart forever.

"Alright, that's enough," I said, pushing him away. "You'll start as my assistant in two weeks."

I walked up the stairs of my garage with a plate of food. I looked at my phone's security feed to ensure Kierra wasn't near the door.

"*Alexa, unlock safe room.*"

The doors opened, and I stepped into the room. I had repurposed the entire space to provide all control from the outside, rather than the inside.

Kierra was sitting in the corner, arms crossed.

I walked over to her and knelt down with the food.

"How are you feeling today?"

"I'm not doing your forced therapy sessions." She took the tray. "So don't even bother."

"I'm not going to keep you here without some sort of rehabilitation," I said. "Let me help you."

"Dr. Harper, you aren't God," she said. "You're not the police. You're not the criminal justice system. You're not a prison."

"I understand that," I said. "But I've worked with the Cluster-B disorders extensively, and I think I could help you feel better. If you try focusing on your emptiness, and boredom—"

"You're like a broken record." She chewed her food noisily. "Emptiness, boredom, emptiness, boredom... I keep telling you, I don't want to change. You think my condition is a bad thing, but it makes me better than everyone. Better than you."

"Don't you want to know what real love feels like?" I said. "Vulnerability, softness, freedom?"

"You first, doctor."

Her eyes met mine – wide and unrelenting.

The sociopath stare.

I held her gaze, determined not to lose this battle of dominance.

"You're good, Dr. Harper," she said. "But you have a weakness."

"And what's that?"

"You don't let reality play out the way it wants to," she said. "You keep trying to arrange and control everything. But sooner or later, reality will win – and the floodgates will open."

"Floodgates?"

"You know I'll get out of here someday," she said calmly. "And when that happens, I will make Lucas mine again."

I accidentally blinked, sealing the fate of our staring contest.

End of Patient File #109

117

A Note on Lucas

Now you know the truth about Lucas – or Noah – which means you finally have all the information you need to read Patient File #220.

I must warn you, it doesn't paint me in a good light. At all. So before you proceed, all I ask is that you remember the good things I've done too.

I care about people. I really do. I just get... agitated. And then I make bad decisions that come back to haunt me.

Unfortunately, this one also came back to haunt someone I care about.

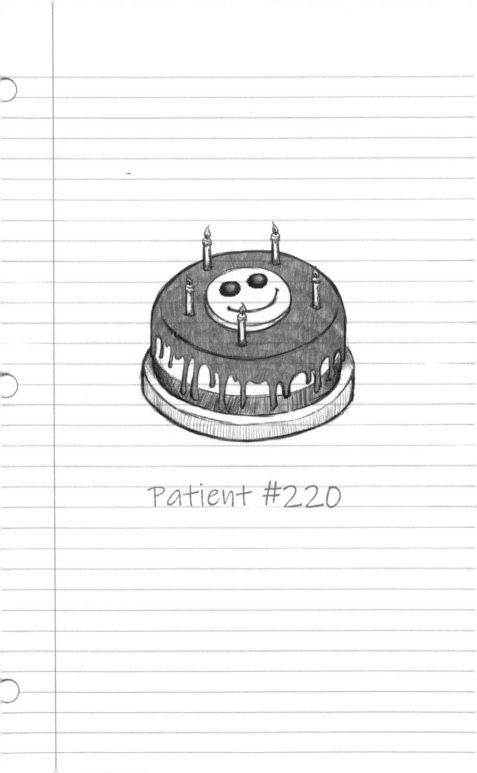

Patient #220

Patient #220

PART ONE

As Officer Donahue finished punching himself in the face, I inched toward the desk drawer – where I kept my gun.

"I'm– I'm so sorry," he said, staring at his fists in disbelief. "I don't know what came over me."

I slowly pulled away from the desk and eyed him curiously.

"Officer, have you had episodes like that in the past?" I asked.

"I think so." His breathing was labored. "Yes."

"And do you recall what triggers them?"

He gazed at the wall for a moment, then he turned back to me and whispered:

"*You have to stop me.*"

"Stop you from what?" I asked, heart pounding.

"Please." His forehead was beading with sweat. "In a few seconds, I'm going to forget. And then I'm going to do it again. It's the only way I can save the drowning girl."

"Officer, stay with me," I said gently, leaning forward. "I apologize if I've misread things, but are you the – the person on the news?"

He froze and held his breath. Then let out a very pained nod.

Aside from his personality, it made a lot of sense. Officer Donahue was a strong man, so he could easily overpower young adults. And with a cop car, he'd be able to convince pretty much anyone to trust him.

"Okay," I said, trying to appear calm. "That's okay. And what's going on through your mind right now?"

"It all started when my daughter went missing last year," he whispered.

He reached into his pocket and handed me a locket. I opened it up and saw a younger Officer Donahue, and a beautiful little girl – no older than 10 or 11.

I handed the locket back to him.

"I'm so sorry," I said. "I had no idea."

"Ever since she disappeared, I keep having these visions." He swallowed. "But I swear to God, they're real. A young girl is drowning, and she's begging for my help."

"What happens next?" I asked.

"There's no time," he said desperately. "You have to stop me, *right now*. Can't you think of some dangerous diagnosis and have me hospitalized?"

I do tend to think about diagnoses pretty quickly, but this was too fast. I didn't know anything about his personal life. His missing daughter could have triggered any number of psychological traumas.

It could be Dissociative Identity Disorder. I know I keep guessing that, and I keep being wrong. Probably because 99% of the time, their alters aren't violent. Sure, there are barriers between alters, but that doesn't mean they blackout and forget a murderous rampage. Blackouts are actually extremely uncommon with DID.

The other possibility was Cotard's Delusion. But that was almost too perfect. A condition where the patient literally believes they are the walking dead. And typically that manifests as anxiety and depression, not cannibalism.

Which brings me to cannibalism. It's not a psychological disorder, although there are obviously mental issues that drive the compulsion and desire to eat another human being. Most often, a euphoric sexual high – or a surge of power. A relief from some sort of void.

"Officer, what goes through your mind when you – bite a person?"

He looked at me and frowned. "What are you talking about?"

I felt chills run down my spine. All of his panic and agitation was gone. Even his tone of voice sounded different.

"What we just discussed," I said. "Your... issue."

"With my wife?" he said with a snort. "We don't bite each other. Not yet at least!"

Knots started to turn in my stomach.

"Officer, you just told me that you're..." I let out a nervous sigh. "You said you're The Zombie."

He looked at me for a moment and then burst out laughing. "Good one, Elliot," he said. "Was that your big theory?"

"No, I'm serious," I said. "You asked me stop you. You said you were going to forget."

He got a weird look on his face and stood up from the couch. "Alright, I don't know if this is your idea of a joke, but it's pretty damn unethical."

"No, please–" I said. "Please sit down so we can talk."

"We're done here," he said, pushing past me.

"I have to call the police," I said. "I have to report you."

He spun around and leaned forward so his eyes were mere inches from my own. "I *am* the police. You're already the laughingstock of the force, Elliot. You think they're going to believe anything you say?"

I bit my lip. There was a really good chance he was right.

"Please," I said, trying one more time to resolve this peacefully. "I know you can't remember, but you told me you're going to hurt more people unless I stop you."

He lowered his voice. "You need to shut the fuck up before someone hears you and takes it seriously."

"It *is* serious!"

"That's enough," he said, turning away. "Next time you need help with your ridiculous patients, don't call 911."

I watched him approach the door. My heart felt like it was on fire as I glanced from the door to the desk. And then I did something very stupid.

I lunged for the gun in my drawer and held it at him. "Put your hands up!"

"What the—"

"Don't even think about it," I said, pointing at the gun on his belt. "Take it off and put it on the ground."

"Elliot, you do *not* want to do this…" he said darkly. "You're pointing your gun at a cop right now. Do you have any idea—"

"Put it on the ground!" I barked.

He shook his head and slowly did as I said.

"Now, we're going to walk to my car," I said, moving close to him so I could reach under his coat and push the gun into his side. "And when we pass by my assistant, you're going to pretend everything is fine."

He glared at me, but started moving with me in an awkward embrace.

"Hey Doc! Hey Officer!" Noah bolted up from his desk. "Need any water or coffee?"

Then he noticed our strange embrace and raised his eyebrows.

"No, thank you," I said quickly, shuffling forward with Officer Donahue. "We just had a great session, and now we're going to get some lunch. Can you please cancel my afternoon sessions and lock up the office before you head home?"

"Okay, sure…" he said. "Is everything okay, doc?"

"Yes," I said with a forced smile. "We're just working on The Zombie case together."

"Oh, wow!" he said. "Okay, good luck."

I let out a sigh of relief. But just as we made it to the front door, Noah spoke again.

"Doc…?"

Come on, Noah…

"Yes?" We turned around.

"What are you doing for your birthday tomorrow?" he said eagerly. "You don't have any appointments, so I was thinking it could be fun to take you bowling!"

"I don't celebrate my birthday," I said. "I'm just going to stay home and do some things around the house. I'll see you on

Monday."

His cheeks went pink and I felt bad, but we needed to get the hell out of here.

"Come on," I muttered to Officer Donahue, pushing him out the door.

I nearly tripped over Kierra's old sneakers as I marched Officer Donahue up the garage stairs. I really needed to get rid of those. It wasn't like she'd be leaving any time soon.

"Alexa, unlock safe room," I spoke into my phone.

"*Okay, unlocking safe room.*"

The door clicked open and I walked Officer Donahue inside. He saw Kierra in the corner and muttered, "What the hell have you gotten yourself into, Elliot ?"

Kierra looked up and raised her eyebrows.

"Wow, another guest at Harper's Hotel of Horror?" she said. "Do most therapists kidnap their patients, or is this just one of your special perks—"

"Kierra, please be quiet," I said, tying Officer Donahue to the opposite corner.

"He burns his dick you know," she called over to him.

"Kierra, be *quiet.*"

"Who is this guy anyway?" she said. "Looks like a cop. Or is it roleplay? Oooh... I bet he's some sort of male hooker that you can force to suck your burnt—"

"He's a cannibalistic serial killer." I stormed over to her with the gun. "So unless you want me to give your new roommate a knife and fork, *SHUT THE FUCK UP AND LET ME THINK.*"

Her eyes went wide. And finally, for a few blissful moments, Kierra stopped taunting me.

I walked back to Officer Donahue and began emptying his pockets. Phone, wallet, keys... I took them all.

I stomped on his phone to destroy any signal. My home was like a digital Fort Knox. But digital security has a major flaw. It can be hacked from the outside. That's why I designed mine on an *intra*-net, not the internet. Meaning, you have to physically be inside my home to access the network. So, definitely no electronics allowed for my guests.

"I'm going to go get some supplies at the hardware store," I said. "To build a partition between the two of you, so you can roam freely."

"Wow, so generous of you…" Kierra muttered.

"No bullshit when I'm gone," I said, ignoring her. "I have a hidden camera in here, so I can see everything you do."

As I made my way back to the stairs, I looked around the room one last time.

Two prisoners living above my garage.

Officer Donahue was right.

What the hell had I gotten myself into?

On my way downstairs, I cursed as I almost tripped on Kierra's shoes again. So this time, I brought them down with me and threw them in the trash.

The following evening, I was reading a book in my living room – occasionally monitoring the video feed to my garage.

The partition was built, so they didn't have to be tied up anymore, which made me feel slightly less psychotic. But my nerves were still on high alert, like my entire body was tensed up.

So when my doorbell rang, I nearly jumped out of my seat.

I reached for my gun and checked the front door camera.

"*Noah…?*" I frowned.

I hurried to the hallway and opened the door.

There was Noah, standing there with a cake.

"Happy birthday, doc!"

"Noah, what are you doing here?" I said. "I told you I don't do birthdays–"

"I know you don't celebrate," he said quickly. "But this isn't a birthday cake. It's just a happiness cake!"

I looked at the cake and saw that he was technically correct. No birthday message, just a lopsided smiley face made of icing. "Noah…"

"Come on, doc!" he said. "No one should be alone on their birthday. Let's just have one slice, then I promise I'll head out."

I glanced up to the garage behind him. This was wrong on so many levels. I was literally holding his ex-wife prisoner a few yards away.

He gave me a smile and inched closer to the door.

I sighed and motioned for him to come inside. "Just for a few minutes."

"Oh, I got you something!"

Through a mouthful of cake, Noah handed me a small wrapped gift that he had been hiding under his jacket.

I reluctantly took it from him and started unwrapping. Inside, I was surprised to find a framed photograph of us.

I raised my eyebrows "Did you… print this out from our company website – on the Staff page?"

"Yeah, it's the only picture of us together!" he said brightly. "I hope you like it."

"Thanks," I said. "This is really thoughtful."

"Wait, where does this go!" Noah jumped up from his seat, running over to the spiral staircase by the living room.

"To the roof," I said. "It's supposed to be an observation deck. I really like stars and constellations, and the skies are very clear out here–"

"Cool!" he said. "Can we go up?"

"Noah, it's freezing out."

"Just for a few minutes!"

"Okay," I said, leaving behind my empty plate. "Alexa, unlock observation deck."

"*Okay, unlocking observation deck.*"

"It's like we're in Star Trek!" said Noah, hurrying up the stairs.

I trailed after him and joined him on the deck.

"Woah…" He leaned against the railing and gazed out across the night sky. "Is that the big dipper?"

"Yes," I said, walking up next to him.

"Is that the biggest constellation?"

"No," I said, pointing to the south. "See that line of faint stars, zigzagging back and forth?"

He squinted for a few moments and then nodded. "I think so!"

"That's the hydra," I said. "It's the largest – and longest – constellation. From Greek mythology."

For the next ten minutes, Noah asked questions and I pointed across the sky to find answers for him.

Somehow, we started talking about past patients – the good ones. The ones who inspired us, challenged us, and gave us hope.

Before I knew it, the "few minutes" had once again turned into much more than that.

Then Noah turned his focus from the stars to me. "Doc, what's your dream in life?"

"My dream?" I laughed.

"Yeah, like what would make you the happiest?"

"I don't know," I said. "To keep helping people, I guess. But sometimes it feels like the hydra… You solve one problem, then you accidentally create two more in its place."

"Yeah, you work with some really scary people," he said. "Doesn't it ever get to you? Always wondering if they're trying to trick you… Always living on edge?"

"That's the job."

"But wouldn't it feel good to have someone take care of you for once?" he asked quietly. "To be with someone who just wants you to be happy – where you know you're totally safe? That way you can finally relax?"

"I don't know," I said again. The idea of someone taking care of me made me extremely uncomfortable, so I changed the subject. "What's your dream?"

"A home in the mountains," he said instantly. His eyes lit up.

"One kitten and two shelter dogs – so they can raise the kitten as a dog. And family dinners for sure. Then after dinner, tucking the kids into bed with a story. Oh! And a big bubble bath on the back deck, to watch the sunset over the mountains"

When he spoke, it was almost as if he painted the stars with his dreams. He was so full of life and energy.

"Your dream is a lot better than mine," I mumbled.

"You can share it with me if you want."

His face immediately went red as he realized what that sounded like.

"Sorry–" he said. "I didn't mean–"

I blushed too. We stood there for a while without speaking.

And then he turned to me, his breath fading to crystals in the cold night air. He gave me a nervous smile and stammered, "Can I– Can I kiss you?"

Suddenly, I felt that old nostalgic warmth come flooding through my heart. Like the breaking of a dam that somehow wiped out all of my rigid defenses.

"Okay," I said awkwardly.

He leaned in, and his soft lips met mine. His kiss was so gentle, and so caring. In that moment, I felt like I didn't have to be Dr. Harper anymore. I could just be Elliot.

I opened my eyes just as he opened his. He gave me an anxious smile, and I smiled back.

But then behind him, I saw a flicker of light from the garage window. My body went cold. *What the hell.* They shouldn't have access to the lights.

And just like that, all of my old defenses came rushing back. What the fuck was I doing? Noah trusted me, and I kept all of these secrets and lies from him. I was just another monster in his life.

I stepped back. "Noah, you need to leave."

His face sank. "I'm sorry," he said. "Did I– Did I do something wrong?"

My phone started buzzing from my pocket.

"No," I said quickly. "It's not you. Please, you just need to go."

He winced, almost as if my words had physically pained him.

I felt more buzzing, so I opened my phone and saw a bunch of security alerts: *SOFTWARE BREACH*. I checked the video feed quickly – Kierra and Officer Donahue were still there. Thank God. But something still felt very wrong.

I practically shoved Noah down the spiral staircase and out my front door.

He turned to me one last time.

"Doc, I– I'm really sorry." His eyes were burning red. "If there's something I did wrong, please tell me. I promise I can fix it–"

"Noah, go."

"Can I still work for you?" he asked desperately, eyes pleading.

"I don't know," I said hastily. My phone buzzed with more alerts. "You need to leave. Now."

I didn't even realize how awful that sounded, until I saw the light leave his eyes as he walked away.

And that was my last memory of Noah.

But I didn't have time to ruminate about that. Something was going on in my garage, and I needed to make sure everything was safe. I closed the door and said, "Alexa, lock all doors."

"Okay, locking all doors."

Then I sat down in the kitchen and opened up my laptop. The screen was a lot bigger, so it was easier to see what was going on. Officer Donahue was sitting and eating in his corner. And–

Suddenly, I felt the blood leave my body.

Kierra was gone.

"Oh my god, Noah…" I whispered out loud. I sprinted to the window to see if his car was still in the driveway.

It wasn't.

I took out my phone and called him.

Then I heard a ring from the living room. I ran over and saw Noah's phone sitting on the couch, right where he had left it.

"Fuck." I kicked over a nearby lamp. "FUCK!"

I opened up my phone and dialed 911 as I hurried to find my

car keys. I knew I'd be arrested, but that didn't matter. They had to find Kierra before she got to Noah. I had left him in such a horrible, vulnerable state.

"Sir, if you're calling about The Zombie news, we cannot provide any additional details at this time," said the operator. "All we know is that a suspect has been taken into custody, and the Police Department is confident that the community is now safe."

What the fuck?

If The Zombie had been captured, then who the hell was in my garage?

I looked back to the security feed and saw Officer Donahue slowly look up at the hidden camera, almost as if he knew exactly where it was. Then he held the locket to his mouth and muttered something inaudible.

And then, without my prompting, Alexa began speaking from my phone.

"Okay, turning lights off."
"Okay, unlocking all doors."

PART TWO

The lights in my house went dark.

Trying not to panic, I spoke into my phone: "Alexa, turn on lights and lock all doors."

"*I'm sorry, I don't recognize your voice profile*," she responded. "*Please login to your account and—*"

"Useless fucking garbage," I snapped. I locked my phone and ran upstairs to get my gun. I've lived here long enough to navigate without the lights.

But just as I got to the bedside table, I felt a sharp prick in my neck, followed by a sudden dizzy feeling. Then a woman's voice whispered into my ears:

"*You need to be quieter, doctor.*"

It wasn't Kierra.

———————————————— // ————————————————

My eyes struggled to open and I couldn't move my body.

I saw three figures wandering around the bed.

"Elliot," spoke Officer Donahue. "Good, you're awake."

"What the hell is going on?" I said groggily.

"Elliot, it's been a while!"

My stomach lurched as the moonlight illuminated the two other figures in my bedroom.

Anne and Rose...

The stabbing sisters from the *My Happy Family* cult – the ones who brainwashed Phil.

I shut my eyes. What in the name of God was happening?

"Oh, don't be shy," Anne spoke. "We're just here to say *thank you*."

"Officer Donahue," I whispered desperately. "I'm sorry I

accused you of being The Zombie. I was wrong. But you have to listen to me, these women are not who you think they are."

He let out a booming laugh. "Elliot, for once in your career, would you stop jumping to conclusions and *listen?*"

"Dr. Harper, you reported our forum to the site administrator last year!" Rose swooped over and kissed Officer Donahue on the forehead. "My husband!"

I thought back to when I first reported the cult. Officer Donahue was the one who took my call and interviewed me. I told him everything – except the messages I posted encouraging Anne and Rose to keep stabbing each other.

"After we talked, I started going through our forum logs," he said. "I noticed an unusual pattern of posts from brand new members – all of them telling my wife and her sister to hurt each other."

"How strange," I said.

"Nasty liar!" shouted Rose, digging through a bag on the ground.

"Needless to say, I stopped them from further harm," Officer Donahue continued. "And we moved the forum, just to be safe. But never in a million years would I have guessed that a *therapist* was posting those messages."

I let out a sigh. "How did you find out?"

"That cow patient," he said. "When I was searching your property, I found a familiar pair of shoes on your garage stairs. I tried to go upstairs, but it was locked up like a goddamn bank vault. Soundproof too. And then I started wondering… what if *you* were the one who kept screwing with our community?"

I tilted my head. "Kierra is your daughter?"

"Yes, in a way…" he said. "Years ago, Rose and I were having trouble conceiving–"

"Oh, come on…" My head was spinning. "Don't tell me she's your fucking *investment?*"

"That's right," he said proudly. "Kierra was the reason we founded *My Happy Family* – to share our success with others. And now people around the world can use our methods to build relationships with friends, children, and romantic partners."

"Success?" I repeated. "All you did was brainwash a child."

"When Kierra turned 18, we told her the truth," he said. "She wasn't even angry with us. She was proud to be a part of our family."

"That's because the alternative would be to face the truth of what you did to her," I said, feeling pity for Kierra for the first time in ages. "That kind of cognitive dissonance would destroy anyone."

"Kierra admires what we do," he said. "In fact, she decided to build a family of her own."

I leaned back into the bed. "You're all fucking insane."

"I must say, her grooming technique is unique," he continued, ignoring me. "It doesn't involve any physical violence. It's purely psychological."

"Wait a minute," I said. "The girl in your locket couldn't have been any older than 12. Kierra is in her 20's."

"It was an old photo – from when we first picked her up," he said simply.

I shook my head in disbelief. "But... you were punching yourself."

"Elliot, your ego knows no bounds," he said. "All I had to do was pretend to be The Zombie. I knew you wouldn't be able to resist the idea of single-handedly stopping the country's most notorious serial killer."

My heart sank. "You're a cop," I said. "Why didn't you just get a warrant to go into my garage?"

"Because of your nasty patient files!" Rose shrieked. "All of your evil little notes... They make our darling Kierra – and our entire community – sound like a bunch of sick freaks. It's a smear campaign!"

"Is it really a smear campaign if it's true...?" I muttered.

"Nasty!" She slapped me across the face. "We wiped your assistant's iPad, but my husband noticed you kept a physical folder on you at all times."

I groaned as I saw her flip through the patient files that I kept locked away in my home office.

Officer Donahue handed my phone to Anne and spoke

quietly. "Delete all of the old security footage from your time with Phil. We can't have anyone tracing this back to us."

Then he turned to me.

"I have to hand it to you, it was unusually difficult to get in here," he said. "We're actually quite good at circumventing security, but we couldn't even make it past your firewall. Your whole network is disconnected from the public internet. It's pretty clever actually."

"Well…" I said dully. "Clearly not clever enough."

"Not against this little doohickey." He waved the locket in my face. He flipped it open and revealed some sort of circuit board under the photo. "Alexa, turn the stove up to high."

Suddenly, I heard my voice speak from the locket: "Alexa, turn the stove up to high."

"*Okay, turning the stove up to high.*"

"Fantastic…" I grumbled. People already think I have a problem with women, so it's almost poetic that Alexa would be my fucking downfall.

"These are cute doodles, Dr. Harper!" exclaimed Rose, holding my patient files out to me. "Is this what you do when your patients are asking for your help?"

"I *do* help," I hissed. "I helped Lucas escape from your bitch of a fake daughter—"

"NASTY!" Rose slapped me again, this time much harder. "And did you say… Lucas? Don't you mean *Noah*?"

My eyes went wide. Rose noticed and smiled.

"That's right, Dr. Harper," she said. "Tonight, Kierra reclaims her investment."

I felt a sudden burst of adrenaline and bolted up from the bed. I tried to hit Rose in the face, but I stumbled from the drugs and accidentally punched her in the boob. She screamed in a strangely erotic way.

Officer Donahue restrained me and shoved me back down to the bed. He injected another dose – of whatever the hell that was – into my neck.

I felt my body go limp again.

"Enough, Elliot…" said Officer Donahue calmly.

"Enough."

I watched in horror as Rose and Anne lifted two huge butcher's knives from their bags.

"Are you going to kill me?" I croaked, trying to keep my eyes open.

"No, you're not getting off that easy," said Officer Donahue. "You've been a real pain in the ass, Elliot. First you took their investment, then you took our daughter and her investment... And do you have any idea how long it took me to move the website?"

"So... What are you going to do to me?" I said weakly.

He looked at me one last time before walking out of the room. "Ladies, get started."

And then, just like a Facebook year-in-review video, Anne and Rose lifted their knives and started driving the blades into each other's torsos.

The last thing I remember from that night was laughing. Yes, laughing. Maybe it was the drugs, but I'm pretty sure my mental state was fine.

I had a chance at real happiness tonight, and I sabotaged it with my own reckless decisions. I don't believe in karma, but I do believe in logic. And logically speaking, if you do enough bad things, one of them is bound to catch up with you in the end. So because of logic, I had no one to blame but myself for whatever was about to happen next.

As they continued stabbing each other, my eyes quivered shut in defeat. But before losing consciousness, I managed to hum to myself:

"Happy birthday, Elliot."

PART THREE

"This was my son, Alex." The school shooter's sobbing mother shared photos with the jury of her dead son's body draped over mine. "He sought help from Dr. Harper, and this is what happened to him."

Moments later, the television at the front of the courtroom started playing home security footage of me kissing my younger male assistant.

"Oh, what the hell does that have to do with anything?" I snapped.

"Doctor, be quiet," my lawyer whispered urgently. "Please."

I settled back into my chair, heart racing.

And for the next two hours, I watched a steady stream of videos, evidence, and testimony that made my practice look like something out of a horror movie.

Next up was Officer Donahue, talking about how I accused him of being The Zombie and locked him above my garage with his missing daughter. He started crying as he told the courtroom that her ex husband – the assistant I kissed – had kidnapped his beautiful daughter.

"I think Dr. Harper and Lucas – or Noah – fell in love," Officer Donahue spoke tearfully. "So they decided to get rid of Kierra, that way they could take her life insurance payout and start a new life together, hence the name change."

"For fuck's sake–"

"Doctor, *be quiet*." Something about the way my lawyer said that made me question if she was even on my side.

There was unending video footage showing Kierra locked above my garage, sometimes soiling herself from those goddamn gummy bears. Someone in the jury let out a sob. There was also video footage of Officer Donahue in captivity, but none with the locket.

They edited out every single piece of evidence that could have gone in my favor.

Then there was Jane's written complaint to the board of psychology about how I blackmailed her husband into therapy. The phone company provided the call transcript. Apparently she redacted it, but that didn't matter anymore. The complaint was one of many anyways.

But the nail in the coffin for my case was Anne and Rose.

The sobbing sisters showed the jury their fresh knife wounds, blathering on about how I held them captive and stabbed them every time they misbehaved. My fingerprints were all over the knives, and they planted that terrifying man-with-two-knives body armor in my closet.

Let's face it. I looked like a fucking psycho.

You might think that some of my happier patients would come testify in my favor, but Phil and Eleanor were long gone by this point – with their phones disconnected to hide from the cult. And there was no way Mormon Jane and Howard would be showing their faces at this shitshow. I don't blame them. The prosecutors and media had done a fantastic job of branding me as the next Doctor Kevorkian.

Plus, between Officer Donahue's police background and *My Happy Family's* talent for video editing, the entire world had become victims of a digital hallucination.

So that left Noah.

I had no idea where Noah was, but he obviously didn't kidnap Kierra. I'm pretty sure he would have shown up here if he could, which meant Kierra probably got to him. And that's what keeps me up at night, more than anything else in this stupid trial.

Long story short, the only real witness to the defense was myself. And what was I supposed to say? "I was framed by a cult leader cop posing as The Zombie killer"? Or maybe... "These sisters actually stab each other to manipulate homeless people!" Or how about, "This cop's fake daughter threatened to drive her ex-husband to suicide." And of course, my get-out-of-jail-free card: "Jane's husband thought he was a cow."

Anything I said would only make things worse. The jury –
and the rest of the world – had already made up their minds.
So I did exactly what my lawyer suggested.
I kept my mouth shut and prayed for a deal.

"Tony, what was your childhood like?"
"It was wild, doc!" he said. "Like nothing you can imagine.
My mom was a hooker, and my dad smacked the shit out of us
every night."
"I'm really sorry to hear that," I said. "But it's never too late
to start healing old wounds."
"Wait, you're not some kind of government agent, are you?"
Tony's eyes went wide. "I've heard about those CIA
experiments where they learn everything about you – just so they
can force you to assassinate the President."
I looked at my cellmate for a moment, and then wrote
something down in my notebook. I guess that's why everyone
around here called him 'Tinfoil Tony'.
"No, Tony," I said gently. "I'm just a therapist who's trying
to help."
"A therapist *in prison?*" he said skeptically. "That really
sounds like some CIA shit. Hey, were you part of the Newtown
cover up?"
"Look," I said, trying to mask my disgust. "I just got here
and I'm terrified. The only way I know how to relax myself is to
help people."
"You think you're terrified now?" said Tony darkly. "Give it
some more time. This place is evil."
"Well, jail isn't supposed to be fun."
"It's not a regular jail." He leaned forward and lowered his
voice. "Sure, some of the inmates are bad – like that Zombie
dude. But it's the innocent ones that'll keep you up at night."
"Everyone says they're innocent," I laughed. "That's my
story too, and yet I held two people captive above my garage."
"This is different," he said. "People pay big money to have

their enemies locked up here. One of the guys on death row was actually a *victim* of violent assault. His ex kept him locked up as a sex slave, and then turned the whole thing around on him."

I screwed up my face. "What?"

"If you think *that's* strange, just wait until you hear about the guards."

I shook my head. Why was I entertaining the words of someone who was so clearly paranoid?

"What about them…?" I said with a sigh.

He lowered his voice again, to the point where it was barely audible.

"The guards are running a pedo-ring in here," he whispered. "That's the real conspiracy."

I glared at Tony, and then walked over to the cell door so he wouldn't see my eyeroll.

As I gazed at the cells around me, I realized that these people made my past patients look like harmless butterflies. It used to be OCD, PTSD, and boanthropy. Now, I was surrounded by mass murderers, rapists, and pedophiles.

My deal was life without parole – in exchange for taking the death penalty off the table.

The only way I would ever feel comfortable in this place was by learning everything about everyone. The inmates and the guards. So what better place to start than with my cellmate?

If this was my fate, I was determined to make the best of it.

And as for Noah's fate?

I've had a private investigator searching for him for weeks. The media is still convinced he kidnapped Kierra, but I know that's not true. I don't even know if he's alive anymore.

I had pretty much given up all hope for finding him. Until one afternoon, I returned to my cell and found something on my bed…

A very peculiar note.

End of Patient File #220

Will you go
to prom with
me?

Yes ☐

No ☐

If we're going to escape, we need to gain the trust of several key guards and inmates. I will explain more soon, but only if you're interested in helping. Please RSVP at your earliest convenience, and leave your response in the head of the broken shower.

Take care.

I looked up from the note and frowned. Was this some kind of joke? Maybe a test from the guards to see if I would say yes?

"Based on the handwriting, I would say *Yes* if I were you," Tony spoke again. "Don't worry, I won't tell anyone your secret."

I shook my head and walked back to the cell door. Looking out across the prison population, I couldn't imagine teaming up with any of them. These were some seriously scary people, and I didn't believe for one second that this note-writer was innocent.

"Who's this guy?"

I turned around to see Tony holding the only photo I had in here.

"Give me that!" I marched over and snatched it from him.

Then I stared at the photograph, even though I had already looked at it a hundred times since I got in here.

It was the one Noah had framed for me.

In the picture, I looked like a bit of a mess. I hadn't shaved in a week, and I had forgotten my contacts so I was wearing glasses. But I still liked the picture, mainly because of Noah's expression.

I was trying to get him to focus on the photographer, because he kept staring off into space and talking about flying sailboats. I got pissy as usual, so the end result was actually a pretty good representation of our time together.

"You're in love with him," said Tony with a toothy grin. "Don't worry, it's all good with me. I'm an ally."

I looked up at him incredulously. "So you think school shootings and mass genocide are false flags, but you're an LGBT ally. That's... special."

"Gotta stand up for love, doc." Tony opened up a crossword

Secret Admirer

I picked up the note and read it curiously.

Will you go to prom with me?

Then there were two checkboxes for "Yes" or "No".

"*What the hell?*" I muttered. Was this some sort of prison bitch thing? My goal here was to learn from my past – lay low and not make any enemies. How had I already upset someone?

"It's urine…" Tinfoil Tony spoke from his bed. "Invisible ink, like the Nazi prisoners used – if you believe that the holocaust happened."

I spun around. "Did you read it?"

"Maybe…" He raised his eyebrows. "Seems that you've made a friend, doc."

He leaned forward and handed me a lighter. I hesitated. I really didn't want to get into trouble, but I already had a life sentence. What was the worst that could happen?

I flicked on the flame and held it safely below the note until words began to appear. In a few more seconds, the entire message was illuminated:

Dr. Harper,

You don't know me, but I know you. I'm sure we'll cross paths soon enough. I followed your trial with keen interest. And I couldn't believe my good fortune when I read that you had been transferred here.

As it turns out, you and I have something in common:

Neither of us belongs here.

Fortunately, I can get us out of here. But I can't do it alone. You see, I know this place inside and out. I know the security, the guard schedule, and I have blueprints of the entire building. But you have something I don't:

The tremendous ability to manipulate people.

puzzle. "If I knew someone who made my eyes light up like that, I'd pick *Yes* in a heartbeat."

"What does love have to do with the note?"

"You've got a life sentence," he said simply. "If there was a chance you could get out of here and be with him, why wouldn't you take it?"

I thought for a moment. I didn't even know if Noah was alive. But maybe Tinfoil Tony was right. If there was a chance I could get out of here and try to find him, didn't I owe him that? Especially after everything I put him through.

But it was too dangerous. I was supposed to be minding my own business and keeping a low profile. This was the complete opposite of that.

I took another look at the photograph and, almost instantly, I felt that soft sensation come flooding back into my heart. How the hell could a picture do that to me?

I had spent my whole life trying to protect and control everything. And look where it got me. Maybe it was time to bid farewell to the guardian around my heart, and try exploring the soft feeling instead.

I slowly raised my hand to my chest and whispered, *"Tell me what to do, Elliot."*

"You know what to do, doc..." Tinfoil Tony jotted down another word on his crossword puzzle. "Unless you think he could be one of those lizard people... Half of our presidents have been reptilian—"

"Jesus, do you have an off button?" I snapped, walking over to his bed. "I need to borrow your pencil."

He raised his eyebrows.

"You know, you've got a bit of a mood issue, doc..." He handed me the pencil.

"Sorry," I muttered, scribbling my answer on the note. "I've been told I have a short fuse."

He took the pencil back and relaxed into his bed.

"Maybe you need a therapist."

Get The Prison Files Today

I'm a Therapist, and My Patient is In Love with a Pedophile
6 Patient Files From Prison

Now available on Amazon

Thank you for reading the #220 files.
Read the Prison Files to find out what happens next.
Learn more at my private practice:

www.DrHarperTherapy.com

@DrHarperTherapy

Subscribe for new stories and incredible fan art on Reddit:

/r/Dr_Harper

If you enjoyed the book, please consider leaving a review
on Amazon to help others discover my files.

Made in the USA
Middletown, DE
13 July 2020